The Missing will be Found

The Missing will be Found

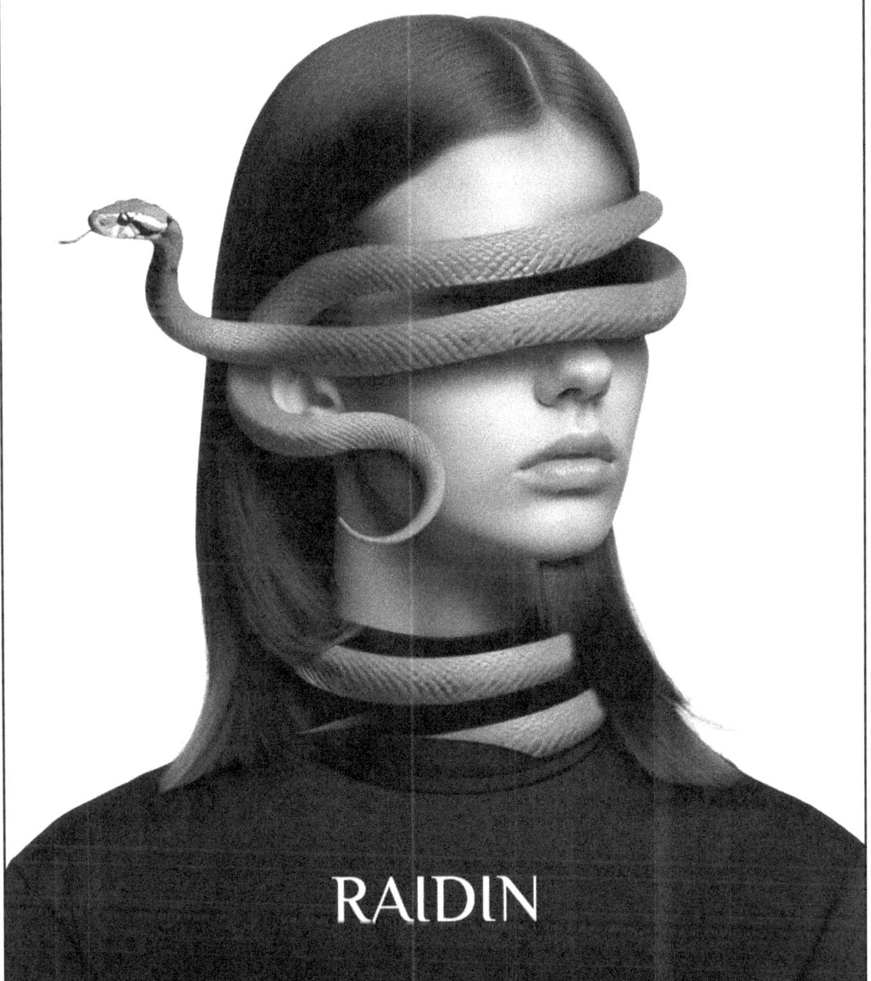

RAIDIN

The Missing will be Found

Copyright © 2024 Raidin

All rights reserved. No part of this publication may be reproduced, stored in any retrieval system, or transmitted in any form or by any means, mechanical, photocopying, recording, or otherwise, without permission in writing from the publisher, except by a reviewer, who may quote brief passages in a review.

This is a work of fiction. All of the characters, organizations, and events portrayed in this novel are either products of the author's imagination or are used fictitiously.

Cover and Interior design by Ted Ruybal
100% Human Made. No AI used.

Manufactured in the United States of America

Wisdom House Books
For more information, please contact:
www.wisdomhousebooks.com

Paperback ISBN: 979-8-218-46814-9
LCCN: 2024915910

YAF000000 | YOUNG ADULT FICTION / General
YAF011000 | YOUNG ADULT FICTION / Coming of Age
YAF003000 | YOUNG ADULT FICTION / Science Fiction /
Apocalyptic & Post-Apocalyptic

1 2 3 4 5 6 7 8 9 10
Second Edition 2024

Dedication

"To everyone who said I should keep writing. To you, who I was sitting next to when I wrote the first words of this book, you know who you are."

Table of Contents

Prologue ix

Chapter 1 1

Chapter 2 7

Chapter 3 15

Chapter 4 25

Chapter 5 37

Chapter 6 45

Chapter 7 57

Chapter 8 63

Chapter 9 73

Chapter 10 93

Chapter 11 117

Chapter 12 121

Chapter 13 137

Chapter 14 145

Chapter 15 177

Chapter 16 201

Chapter 17 217

Chapter 18 237

Chapter 19 245

Epilogue 257

About the Author 267

Readers note:

The title does not lie.

Prologue

2073

      If humanity despised the thought of the world ending, why spend years contemplating on how exactly it would come about? Why focus on such a dismal future when the possibility of the rest of your life was floating at an arm's length away?

Explosions, maybe, some thought. Flooding, loss of food, lack of water, they were all options. Aliens, that one was always interesting. Creatures coming from space, attempting to take us over. Some people hated that thought more than anything, losing their lives as well as freedom. Other people believed that if this were to happen, it would finally bring an end to a lifetime of pain.

Death.

Decay.

They were all wrong.

It makes me laugh, though it probably isn't exactly the most laughing matter. Apologies, let me start over.

It makes me laugh because of how unimaginable it is. I don't blame society for their fear, but I blame them for how long it took that fear to finally unleash. To take over. To cause change. I don't enjoy blaming people, trust me. I'd rather blame myself over anyone else.

Apologies, back to the topic. Which was . . . the end of the world. *Right.* Got it. See, there's a reason why everyone was wrong. The end of the world wasn't terrifying, but the opposite really. No one thought out of the box, or if they did, they were laughed at. Pessimists ruled, but the few optimists held their faith. Who said the end of the world signaled the end of new beginnings?

50 years ago was when the world ended. Or, rather, began. 'Began' is a better word. How do I say this right? *51* years ago was when the world ended. Things got bad, but who was shocked? No one, really. Well, maybe some people. Maybe a lot of people.

From how I understand it, a bunch of things went haywire, starting with water.

Water seems so passive until it realizes it's being wasted, and then it turns quite defensive.

It flooded. A lot.

Climate change. But again, who was shocked?

I just don't understand what went through their minds, there were so many warnings. So many ways to make it right. Religious folk believed it was God's doing, that he was making a second flood for some glorious person to go and make their ark. No one ever did. There was no ark. The flooding was all a consequence, not of God's actions, but humanity's own hubris.

The land followed suit. Food ran short, people freaked out. The temperature rose, people freaked out. Consequences are easy to run from, and who's to say I wouldn't have done the same? I like to think I wouldn't have fled, that I would have been part of the group that changed history. However, part of me knows that maybe I would've stayed in my home, feeling helpless from the inevitability of it all. I can't be blind to my own faults.

Finally, usable water was depleted, and some people actually joined together to fix it. It was the final straw. Water was the start, the end, and the new beginning.

Technically speaking, the world never truly ended, but the world as people knew it *did*. People who were alive at the turning point will tell you that they had no hope. No hope in humanity. No hope in change. Until Petrichor took over, beginning with the water. And this group has been with us ever since. They started small, a group of like-minded people desiring something better of the world. Though they were against the choices that society made, they did not dismiss society itself. They wanted *change*, and they wanted accountability. Though they grew to a decent size, no one expected the extent of their influence. They had solutions. Solutions to everything. Solutions that the governments at the time didn't even think of, or chose to simply ignore. To this day, I don't know how they did it. I don't know how they fixed the water. I don't know how they got people to listen, let alone gain power. All anyone has ever really told me was, "Right people. Right time." And by some miracle, Petrichor was right. About *everything*.

Petrichor rules over everyone now, what is left of the world and its people. In history books, this would've been deemed impossible. At the same time, people in history never saw the world end. Or *almost* end. Great things happen in desperation, depending on who you're talking to. Petrichor had good people, they still do. They made the world beautiful again. They restored hope, acting as a crutch until the world could walk again.

But this is not to say that the world is without problems. There are still groups out there that see the world in a different light. I know that there were some resistance groups, there always are, especially when Petrichor first came to power. In school, we learned about a specific group that did want want anyone ruling at all. They believed that the world no longer wanted us to inhabit it. After everything we did, I wouldn't be surprised. However, unlike this group, Petrichor and its followers believed in second chances. They believed in forgiveness.

There were smaller groups that did not exactly raise resistance, but they were skeptical. I assume it seemed too good to be true, why would Petrichor help everyone without asking for something in return? They didn't even seek power, just assistance from civilians in their mission to fix what had been destroyed. They became the government because that's what the people wanted.

As far as I know, there are no resistance groups anymore. If there are, no one speaks about them. Petrichor, even though its inner workings remain hidden, is rather open about everything except for the fall. They state that there are far more important issues to speak about than their own accomplishments in the past. We learn about the history of the world, the mistakes that humans made, the reconstruction still occurring throughout our country and the world. Petrichor has admitted their past mistakes, such as the breaking of the dam west of my city that flooded three adjacent towns. Four people died, and the government took full blame. I know that might seem small on a world-wide scale, but it meant a lot for the people involved, for our whole area. It showed that we could trust them, that they weren't trying to hide anything. Perhaps I'm biased as the child of two Petrichor employees, but I truly believe that if there were still resistance groups that were causing trouble, Petrichor would tell us. I think people just realized they were in good hands, and they finally accepted it. The government has done nothing except make the Earth a better place."

Chapter One

March 18, 2073

3:30 PM

"" . . . the government has done nothing except make the Earth a better place . . . Ira, this was supposed to be a speech about something you believe in, not a 'let's kiss Petrichor's ass' speech," Grey sighs, sliding the paper towards me.

"Well, I mean, I do believe in it."

He gives me a disappointing glare before standing to leave, "you have your entire break to fix this, and I think you should use it. You write stuff like this all the time, try something new, huh? I love you deeply and you know I love how you write, but you asked for advice, so there you go."

I nod, mentally ripping my words to shreds as he walks out of the library doors. See, I know he's right, I know that all of my past assignments have been similar, but this is what I'm good at. I'm good at writing about the government and everything that they've done. I feel like I could write a whole thesis about how different the world is now compared to then. Before the end, the almost end. Why fix something that isn't broken? Well, Grey would say there's always room for improvement. He's been my friend for years, since before I can remember. Some people have stated that they're surprised at us being friends, and I guess I can see why. We're opposites in many ways.

Grey is outgoing, he's charming, he has more confidence than I've ever seen in one singular person. And god, is he beautiful. Back before the end, there is no doubt he would have been a model. He is my friend, and nothing more, but I can see why he has had so many people wrapped around his finger. Grey lives for that. He loves the chase, the adrenaline, and even the fall, though he would never admit to it. There would be nothing more for him to complain about if he did.

"Grey!" I call, using most of my strength to propel myself forward into the opened doors of the bus. Not only does he like the chase in relationships, but he likes to *be* chased as well.

"Good, you made it!"

"You could have waited."

He puts his hands on my shoulders as we start to move, "you would have stayed in there all day if you could. Personally, I want to go back to school, grab my things, and get the hell out. Start break early. And hey, if we get the job, you'll be in the library all the time."

Grey pulls me closer to him before I can respond. Luckily for him, I relent, allowing his stable body to secure me in turn. I dislike busses much more than metros. The metros are quieter, faster, and their destinations are better as well. The busses only take you around the outskirts of the city, between the three main towns: Apex, Chapel Hill, and Pittsboro. Apex is small, only consisting of necessity shops and a few houses. My parents are usually able to get everything we need straight from Petrichor; food, hygiene projects, what have you. But, very rarely, I ride to Apex for clothes or for other such things. I live in Pittsboro, where most people who live outside of the city are located. Before the end, it used to be rather small, but the government decided to build it up for residential uses. I'm glad they did, it's beautiful. Covered in trees, lakes, ponds; nothing feels wholly man-made, though I know it is.

Finally, there's Chapel Hill, where we are currently. It used to be a college, I believe, which is why it now holds all of the schools in the area, including the city. That is one thing I believe the city kids envy us over, the fact that their ride is much longer than ours to get to school. But, they get to ride the metro. The metro is the only way to get from the towns to the city. One metro for each town, all leading to the station in Raleigh. I love it there, I really do.

According to my classes, there used to be a multitude of different towns surrounding Raleigh, but they slowly got destroyed right before the end and during. These areas are fenced off from the rest of the population, but there's a constant buzz of reconstruction whenever one passes these outdated towns. They're called sustainable blocks, the land under construction, and Petrichor states they'll be done in five years' time. I hope nothing gets delayed, though you never know with projects like this, even if it's under good management. Some things are out of the government's control.

"Ready?"

I finally open my eyes against the red of Grey's sweater, keeping them closed helps with the motion sickness. The bus has stopped finally, and the rest of the small crowd has already made its way to the exit doors.

"Yeah, but after we grab our stuff, I have to head home; my parents are getting off of work early and want to have dinner with me. They're leaving again next week, work trip."

Grey grins as we step off together, "how long are they gone for?"

"No," I shake my head, "just because I have the house to myself doesn't mean you can have Dean over."

"First off, wasn't gonna ask that, I would never—"

He has, multiple times.

"—and second off, I haven't spoken to Dean in almost a week, he's done for, he's toast."

"Right."

No one is ever truly done for in Grey's little world. He would probably get back in contact with someone he had a crush on when he was seven if he could, though he swears he can't remember anyone he liked in his younger years. I wouldn't be surprised if he has them all written down somewhere.

Grey holds the large metal door open as I slip through, trying to make as little noise as possible. Our school is an old brick building, one that does little in order to stop the echoing of even the quietest footsteps. For that reason, everyone tries to stay relatively silent in the hallways in order to not disturb the classes in session. As far as I know, classes now work relatively the same as they did before, just located in a different place. There are multiple different buildings for early schooling, middle school, high school, so on and so forth, but they all reside in Chapel Hill. There are still college classes here, just with a much smaller student population. We lost a lot of people during the end, something that we're still recovering from.

Oh, and also, no more private schools. The Petrichor-made curriculum is the same no matter which school you get placed into. If I were to talk to someone from the Kenan high school, we would know the same things. I think it's better that way, more equal, you know?

But even though we learn equally, that doesn't mean each school functions the same. For example, ours allows each student to pick which season they would like to have free, which helps in terms of applying for jobs, especially if they only hire for specific seasons. We chose to have spring free in order to work in the library, even though undoubtedly most others choose to have their summers off. Personally, I would have wanted to have my autumn free, but my friends insisted on spring, and I gave in.

Grey opens our conjoined locker, holding back the avalanche of papers and trash in order to grab our bags.

"We probably should clean it-"

"Nope," he interrupts before practically running out of the door, ignoring the echo of noise, "I like it like that."

⁊⊚⚏⊙⁊

"They haven't told us how long we'll be away, or exactly what for, all we know is that it's important. They require us," my mother states, shrugging indifferently.

I stab a fork into my noodles, smushing the butter as it slowly begins to melt, "They've never asked either of you to go on a trip before, right? Does that mean it's a good thing?"

I mean, it doesn't seem like a bad thing, especially if Petrichor chose my parents in specific.

My father nods, "We think so."

Before I can stop myself, my mouth is already moving.

"Do you think you'll get to meet the leader?"

Neither one responds.

For some unknown reason, it's almost always been a taboo in

my household to talk about the leader of Petrichor. I assume it's out of respect, or something close to it, that makes my parents so uncomfortable to speak about the subject.

"We'll have to leave our Tirns here," my mother continues, ignoring my question as I slowly shovel buttered noodles into my mouth, "that was their only request." Mom adds.

Meaning the only way I can communicate with them is now no longer an option.

"How come? People used to take their phones with them on business trips back in the old world."

"Tirns aren't phones, Meira, and the old world is gone. Things are different. If they ask us not to bring our Tirns, we won't bring our Tirns."

"I know, but . . . how will I get in touch with you?"

You know, if I needed something; if there was an emergency, all of the above. Anything.

"We won't be gone for long."

Chapter Two

March 21, 2073

10:45 AM

66 Hello, hello, can we get the hell out of here please? Let's go, let's go, let's go!"

Grey's here.

Carefully closing the door behind me, I walk down the front steps, "I'm not the only person that lives here, I know that you're excited but—"

He's smiling from ear to ear, "Well, I wasn't about to go in. I didn't know if your parents had left yet."

Lie.

He has burst into my house uninvited on multiple occasions.

Without his trademark smile, I imagine more people would be intimidated by him. Everything about Grey is sharp, cut like a diamond: eyes, nose, lips, jawline, makeup, clothes. But he looks different today, his blonde hair pulled back into a tight ponytail that just barely grazes the bottom of his shoulder blades; he has been growing it out for what feels like forever. One time, I made him sit down with me to watch one of my favorite old movies and he complained the whole way through. So, in turn, I complained about something he cared about just as much as I cared about the movie: his hair. Not that I don't like his hair, I do, but it was needed to get the point across.

Subsequently, he didn't talk to me for three days. It actually scared me to think he would never talk to me again. Finally, Grey called me on the fourth day; he had lost his phone, that was all.

"Come on, at least acknowledge it!" His hands fly widely, gesturing up and down his torso. I believe he's referring to his jacket, as it would be hard not to acknowledge. A million pieces of small, black-stained glass shards cover the surface, reflecting the sunlight. It's mesmerizing in a way, only adding to his sharpness.

"I like it. You look very professional," I sigh as I look down at my own outfit. I didn't realize we were supposed to dress up for this. Why didn't he tell me? Much like our personalities, I am dressed the exact opposite of him: a simple, blue tank top hanging lightly over my shoulders by two silver chains. Not to mention the jeans. If I was aware we were dressing up, then I would not have chosen pants with holes throughout the legs, matching chains hung in the gaps. The blue top matches the blue laces of my shoes. I was proud of the outfit, if I'm being honest. It reminds me of the fashion before the end, though I guess not much has changed in the clothing world since then. The main difference perhaps would be the availability of items today, such as Grey's jacket for example. If I understand it correctly, a clothing item like that would have not only been hard to find, but it would have been expensive as well. But, like almost everything else, Petrichor found a solution, now it's quite common to see clothes like that.

Grey sighs, "You're not underdressed." He knew what I was thinking.

"But what if—"

"No, not hearing it. I mean, hell, I'm not even wearing shoes."

I look down. He is, in fact, not wearing shoes, or socks for that matter.

"Oh, why aren't—"

Grey interrupts me again by containing me in a loose headlock, "We live in paradise, sweetheart. No need for it."

Despite the lack of seriousness in his tone, he is right. I think we will only be walking through grass today, unless I'm completely wrong about the directions. Grass covers almost everything now, another silver lining from the end, as now it is no longer man and nature fighting for space, but sharing it.

"Why are we going this way?" I ask, walking slowly behind Grey as he starts to disappear behind the forest's edge on our way to the library.

"I've been this way before, I'll be your designated tour guide," he says with a slight bow.

I can't help but laugh with hesitance as Grey reaches his hand out and gestures towards the forest with the other. I have no reason not to take this path, but I'd much rather just go the normal way. I really don't want to be late to the first day of our job, but I don't think anything will convince him otherwise. He's extremely persistent . . . and I can't help but love him.

Reluctantly, I take his hand as he practically drags me towards him. Grey links my arm in his. "Thank you, beautiful."

The grass slowly turns to pine straw under our feet. I'm worried he's going to step on something, but he doesn't seem to mind. The trees loom over us, comfortably intimidating, perhaps like Grey. The early sunlight filters through the leaves perfectly, and in that second, I want nothing more than to capture the moment in a picture.

I assume Grey knows where he's going, or I hope at least. I wish

I could enjoy this walk, close my eyes and relax, but the intense feeling of lateness distracts me.

"The trees are greener now," I whisper, half to myself.

"Hmm?"

I snap back to reality, thinking of an answer, "Sometimes I believe the trees look greener now, more than they did before."

"Before what?" he asks, apparently zoned out as well.

"Petrichor. All of the old pictures; the trees seem different."

Grey squeezes my arm a little, "You talk about before too much."

I sigh, "Never."

"Maybe the trees look worse now. We wouldn't know if Petrichor faked every form of media back then, to make things seem worse," Grey responds.

I don't reply, not because I'm annoyed, but because he could be right.

"Oh . . . sorry, Ira, I shouldn't . . . your parents," he mumbles.

"No, no, you know I'm alright when you say things like that, Grey. You could be right."

He has always questioned Petrichor. Whenever he mentions it, he always feels bad after he remembers that my parents work there. I've never minded when he does it, but I have to repeat that to him constantly. Grey's skepticism comes largely from his grandparents who'd passed years ago. He was never close to them, but it still affected him. They were in their nineties, both alive before Petrichor came to be. Oddly, his grandparents had very little knowledge of almost anything from their past, albeit no noticeable signs of dementia or similar maladies. Many from before suffered the same loss in memory; it wasn't necessarily kept a secret either. Petrichor has been asked about this many times; the answer, at least to me, makes sense. They stated the polluted air from the increase of nitrous oxide was toxic enough to affect the chemicals in the brain, resulting in a form of memory loss. Even with that answer, Grey still doesn't trust it.

We continue to walk, occasionally stopping to look at a bird or a plant while my tour guide spewed completely false information about each. This is not a onetime occurrence; one of Grey's favorite things to do is appear confident in anything far from the truth, especially the promise he made to me about five minutes before that we won't be late. The longer time slips from us, the more anxious I become. The walk is no longer peaceful. I can't do it. I look around, no buildings or people in sight. I feel like we should be getting close by now, but there's nothing but open forest before us.

Suddenly, Grey stops and crouches, yanking me down with him. "Listen," he whispers.

My heart starts to beat faster as I strain my ears against the rhythm. I shake my head before Grey leads me quickly through the underbrush and stops again, remaining crouched. Thorns have started to leave small cuts along my arms, red scratches that threaten my intrusion on nature. I should have brought a jacket. I should have done a lot of things.

"Do you hear it? This is why I wanted to bring you here," he practically squeals, very much too close to my ear.

I listen closely, appeasing his request. At first, there's nothing but the sound of a gentle wind. And then—

"*. . . never shined through . . . I've shown . . .*"

A song plays lightly in the distance from an unknown source. I can barely make out the lyrics.

"It's coming from that way," Grey points, "I've gone closer to it before, the last time I heard it. It's like an abandoned shed of sorts, you know, probably haunted. *Very* haunted . . . I've never heard a song like that."

"Instruments?" I ask.

He nods, "I think so."

See, music isn't exactly banned, it's just different.

It's very hard to find older music now, and the newer songs are all fake, computer generated. No instruments; usually not even a singer. I wish I could find vinyl, I would love that. It seems like it would be addicting to me, watching the record spin.

The needle hitting the grooves . . .

Peaceful.

I realize that Grey is still speaking, ". . . even though no one should be living out here. I think we should go closer."

"What? No. We're probably already late."

He takes out his watch and shakes it near my face, "An hour, my friend, we have an hour."

I sigh, overdramatically on purpose in an attempt to get my point across. He could be completely lying about the time. I wouldn't put it past him.

"Nope, I'm not listening to your whiny ass. Let's go."

We stop barely fifteen feet from the shed, Grey insisting we should stay crouched. The building in front of us is in complete disrepair, pieces of rotted wood scattered everywhere. If it wasn't for the music, it would seem uninhabitable. Speaking of the music, its blaring now; I have no idea how you can't hear it outside of the forest. The area looks almost fake, maybe picturesque; the green bushes growing widely around the foundation, an old wind chime catching the breeze lightly. I want to freeze the scene, fit it into a small square and pin it to my wall. The old world was real, sometimes I forget. Too real.

"So, what's your guess, Ira? Old man, old woman, a group of horny teenagers wanting some privacy?"

Grey's voice cuts through my attempt to save a permanent mental picture as I elbow him in the rib. Grey immediately falls backward, laughing. I hate him, but in the kindest way possible. He's one of my best friends. He knows exactly how to make me hate him.

"Teenagers wouldn't listen to that music, I've never even heard it before," I reply.

"*Mm*, you would."

"I would."

Anything to get closer to the old world. Not to bring it back, not to experience everything that it went through, but to learn. To know. It just seems so real.

"Maybe—"

The music abruptly stops, cutting him off. I barely have time to think before Grey grabs my hand and leads me quickly through the bushes.

It almost feels like my mind shuts off, the red scratches beginning to bleed.

Eventually, we're far enough away where we can stand up fully, which thankfully makes this marathon a lot easier to manage. I barely notice the switch back to grass underneath us before we're bolting out of the forest. Conveniently, we end up right in front of the library. I guess he *did* know where he was going.

The outside of the building is beautiful. Two stories of white brick, a small trickle of a man-made waterfall flows down the right side, next to the main doors. In front, two columns, which I suppose were to made to look Greek, stand in ruin.

Grey bends over to put his hands on his knees, "I hate running."

I wipe the sweat from my face, "Me too."

Chapter Three

⁊⊙▲⊙⹀

March 21, 2073

11:15 AM

66 If you two don't get your asses over here, I swear to god!"

I look to my right, seeing a familiar face standing just in front of the path that Grey and I should have taken to get here. Lara.

Lara is extremely sarcastic and, quite frankly, she usually always means it. She can be kind though, as well as very smart, maybe even more involved in the Petrichor controversy than Grey is. But she never fails to think before she speaks about it, even though again, I would be fine if she did, but I think she believes I do actually mind, somewhere deep down that my thoughts cannot reach.

Not only that, but she has quite the history of showing up late to everything. Bearing this in mind, as well as the fact that she's already here can only lead to one conclusion.

"You said we weren't late!" I whisper frantically to Grey.

"We're not," he remains bent over, "I told her that we had to be here at 11:00 instead of 11:45. Work smarter, not harder."

"I'm not deaf, jackass, and I'm not always late," Lara wipes the hair off of her forehead.

It's short now, much shorter than usual, a bit longer than a pixie cut. She got it done a while ago but I'm still getting used to it. It fits her perfectly, as does her style. She mostly wears sweaters, plaid skirts, and tights, all in a variety of nude colors. It fits her because it contrasts dramatically with her personality, resulting in all of the charm it brings.

"Yes ma'am." Grey replies.

Similarly to Grey, Lara can be rather menacing, and she's also been a friend since before I can remember, but maybe that could be considered obvious based on the way she speaks to us. Today she's wearing a long white jacket that reaches her ankles as well as loose beige pants. Her top is similar to mine except for the color; she looks good.

She always looks good.

I wouldn't be surprised if Lara would have been a model back in the day, just like Grey.

"Grey didn't tell you to dress up, did he?" She's looking me up and down, and I can't tell if it's horror or disappointment in her eyes. Obviously, I hadn't received the memo.

Grey exhales through his teeth, "I thought *you* did."

Lara and I turn on him.

"I told you I wouldn't be able to—"

"*You* said I wasn't underdressed!"

Grey raises his hands in surrender, "Ladies, ladies, please. Lara, my love, I apologize. Ira, you look great. Since we're here early, and I'd rather not be in this situation anymore, can we go in now?"

Lara scowls as my mind spirals into a million different possibilities, roughly focused on my outfit and how whoever's in there will react.

"Fine, Grey, let's go."

He puts his arms around our shoulders as we walk towards the door.

I sigh, "I'm gonna get told to leave."

He squeezes my hand, "The worrier, the partier, and the mean bitch," Grey shoots a look at Lara. "Three peas in a pod, aren't we?"

"You're not gonna get kicked out, Meira," Lara whispers.

I'm thankful for her, for both of them really. Grey makes me laugh and Lara helps me relax. What I contribute to the friend group is left to be determined. I wonder if they need me as much as I need them.

Do they need me at all?

Well.

This building is impressive, inside and out. Extremely impressive.

Before now, I had never been to this library, considering it's sitting in the outskirts of the city; no doubt, it is a lot larger than the one back at Chapel Hill. When we walk in, the temperature seemingly drops almost twenty degrees. Grey makes a joke about keeping the books cold but his words were the last thing I could focus on; I wasn't listening. Lara smacks him on the arm.

The ceiling reaches a lifetime above us, and I crane my neck to take in the view. The sparkle of glass is the only hint that gives away it is in fact a ceiling, not the blue sky in the distance. There's a tall fountain that reflects the sun perfectly across the shelves. The books almost look like they're glowing, beckoning to be read. Speaking of books, they're everywhere. More books than I'd ever seen before, all packed into one ethereal space of knowledge and nature. The shelves are dark brown with vines sliding down the sides, likely fueled by the sun shining through the glass. Unlike the school library, there's no one here that I can see. I know that they only allow certain people in libraries like this one, but despite this, it's amazingly quiet.

It almost seems like we're in a forest with the mix of green, and brown, along with the blue from the fountain water.

And what's a forest without its keeper?

A woman appears next to one of the shelves. She's older, but her eyes don't seem to agree, matching the green of the vines. She's wearing a dark blue dress that stops below her knees. The woman swings around towards us, her silver hair falling to her waist. Beauty in knowledge.

"You're here for work?" she asks. Her voice seems familiar, almost unsettling. Lara nods as the woman takes a moment to look at us, green eyes raking, until she finally meets mine and frowns slightly. Did I already do something wrong? I look down at my outfit, a panic threatening to boil over. *I knew it, I knew I would—*

"I like your shoes," she whispers, melodical as a wind chime.

The panic dissipates and I can't help but smile. She likes my shoes.

"My name is Izmene. No nicknames, please, just Izmene. I want to thank all of you for applying and to give a proper welcome; however, I assume you all would like to know what you will be doing first. Follow me," she winks before quickly turning away. God, she walks fast.

Grey grabs my hand as we practically run to keep up with her, "Milf?" he whispers.

I stifle a laugh as Lara almost knocks him over trying to whisper in his ear, "She's like seventy, Grey!"

"Okay, fine, a *gilf*."

"I hate you," I sigh.

"You hate me because I'm right."

"No, I—"

Izmene stops quickly in front of a dark oak door, "You three are very lucky to work here, especially during spring. I'm not aware if you know this or not, but you were not hired by accident; we have almost a hundred people your age submitting resumes for a job here. You three were picked because of your minds, not your actions. As you know, the credentials to even enter into this building are limited, as the majority of books here were made before the end. Petrichor is many things, but they are not book burners," she smiles oddly, "anyway, your teachers recommended you three, and now you're here. Don't take that for granted." Izmene pauses and turns to me, "Meira, you stay with me. You two can go through this door and they'll tell you what to do."

She speaks almost as fast as she walks. I would believe it if she told me her mind is going at a constant speed that doubles ours.

Lara stiffens, "We were told we would all be able to work together?"

"And you will," she responds.

We all lighten.

"But not today."

Izmene almost pushes Lara and Grey through the door, closing it loudly behind them.

And now I'm alone with her.

Lara was right, we chose this job so that we could be together, and we were told we could. I'm not sure if this was deliberate or just simply a change of plans, but I'm stuck nonetheless.

"I'm sorry about that. You'll forgive me when I show you why," she turns away, shooting me a short smile. I stand for a moment debating on whether or not I should go through the door or follow her. But I need this job. My friends will forgive me.

Right?

"You know what vinyl is, correct?"

My heart skips a slight beat when she speaks that word.

"What?" I snap from my thoughts, trying not to wonder if I'd somehow dragged us all into a living hell.

"Is that a no? Vinyl?" Izmene asks again.

"No . . . sorry," I shake my head to clear my thoughts, "I know what vinyl is."

She studies me. I study myself. Vinyl no longer exists. It was a fragment of the old world, I've never seen one, I've never touched one.

"How do you know?" Izmene whispers.

How . . .

No, she's right. How do I know? I know what vinyl is? Yes. But why is she asking? Honestly, I really wasn't planning on freaking out today. I've always known. I've never seen any pictures; how do I know? The spinning. The needle. The laughing if it spins too fast or too slow. The needle. If it plays backwards.

The needle.

"Meira?" she pauses, noticing the panicked look on my face, "maybe you heard about them when you were younger . . ."

She continues to ramble as I sort out the mess in my mind.

Maybe she's right, maybe someone said something about it before. No, I can picture it. I can picture the record spinning and the needle moving up and down in smooth waves as if a bent album was spinning and how the music scratched, how it sounded so soothing and natural and . . . holy shit. I don't tend to curse a lot but this situation fully deserves it because I'm frustrated, god am I frustrated. I don't understand. Why don't I understand?

I didn't even notice that I was still following her as I was thinking. Nor did I notice that she had led me to a door that she had already opened and . . . It's a room, small, about the size of a relatively large utilities closet. The walls are hidden by stacked wooden crates that cover nearly the whole floor. I can barely step into the room after Izmene.

"Vinyl."

Vinyl.

"Wait . . . vinyl?"

She nods; the twinkle in her eye shining brighter now. "Before you ask, no, Petrichor doesn't know about this and yes, I intend to keep it that way."

Oh. *Oh?*

Is vinyl illegal? No, it's definitely not, I've never heard that. Then why doesn't Petrichor know about this? Also, not only that, but why me? I just wanted a job! I like books, I enjoy learning about the old world! Not this, not like this. Something feels wrong. She feels wrong, this room feels wrong, being separated from my friends feels wrong. I need to ask. I need to ask questions. Why is she showing me this? Why did I get chosen for this?

"Why . . . why don't they know about this?"

Izmene takes a long pause, "Petrichor is very . . . discreet, I'll put it that way. I assume you've wondered how they came to power?"

I have, but she doesn't need to know that.

She continues without my answer, "No one really knows. I don't even know, and I . . . I was there when they did. They haven't done anything wrong, but it's hard to trust something you know nothing about. As for this, these are mine." She gestures around the room, "I've kept them since before the fall. By the fall, of course, I mean before the new beginning. Anyways, no one knows about this, give or take a few. The government trusts me to run this building, they do not do checks here, though perhaps they should."

I wait for Izmene to continue talking but she refrains. You know, I was hoping she would answer at least some of the questions I have. Like, why am I here? Or, do you know where my parents work? So on and so forth. I don't want to ask. I don't really know her that well. Do I have to ask? What if she thinks I'm being rude? She won't. But what if she does? I'm going to ask.

"I—my parents, I'm not going to say anything to them but they do work for Petrichor."

"I know, I know, don't worry. That's partly why you're here; the other part of course being your application and that whole spiel. Your recommenders said you had a special interest in the old world, and even though I'm not sure if they meant it positively, I took it as such. We're transporting these vinyl to different places, places that need them."

She still doesn't explain my part to play in all this, but I decide to ask another question instead.

"Who needs them?"

"People like me. People who remember records but can't find any. The world is better, drastically, but people still need a way to escape. Good music can help people with that. It also might have the potential to allow people to remember things. It didn't, let's say, help me but we're hoping it will help someone else. Maybe then we'll have some answers."

I shake my head, unable to hide my confusion.

"How would music help people remember? The memory loss was caused by air pollution, right? You said we are hoping it would help someone else. Who's we?"

"I understand you'll have many questions about this. First of all, Petrichor told us about the effect of air pollution; I'm not denying that there was air pollution, I can remember that clearly. All I'm implying is that there is a chance the memory loss might not have been fully caused by it. As for your other question, now isn't the time, we only just met."

Of course it's not the time. Whenever someone says that it usually means you're either too young, dumb, or ignorant to understand. Her gaze holds something within it, analyzing, searching for something that I am unaware of.

"Now, Meira . . . can I call you that, or do you go by Ira?"

Such a simple question given the gravity of what she was just sharing with me.

"Either . . . I'm alright with either."

Izmene nods shortly, "I wish for you to help me organize the records, to help me get these vinyl out to people. You would only be in this room, no danger of transporting these and getting caught I assure you. You can tell your friends I assigned you to do inventory in another section, or whatever you like truly, as long as it's not the truth. Can I trust that you'll keep this job to yourself? You don't have to accept the offer, I'm not forcing you, I promise. I realize it is a lot to ask, but part of me feels as if you will want to." She hands me a thin, rectangular card with the number twenty sketched into it. After the fall; I think I'm going to call it that now, it's a good name for it, Petrichor came up with a new form of currency. Don't ask me how it works, that's Lara's expertise. All I know is that a twenty-card equals quite a lot of cash. More than I've ever seen.

"I can't take this, I didn't do anything today."

"It's not a bribe," she laughs. "Tell your friends you did hard work today. We'll talk more another day if you accept the offer. I don't wish to overwhelm you."

Yeah, a bit too late for that.

Izmene closes my hand around the card.

"Thank you," I whisper.

Chapter Four

March 21, 2073

12:00 PM

After I close the large library doors behind me, I make my way back to my house, avoiding the woods with a wide berth. Too much has happened today, my thoughts begin to whisper as my ears involuntarily attempt to hear any hints of music coming from behind the tree-line. Nothing. Today felt like one large test to see which world I'm loyal to, the perfect one I currently live in, or the twisted fallen one, the one that got what it deserved. In my right mind, I would choose my current life, but there is always something calling me, showing me that there is so much left to learn about the world that had died for its sins. Apparently, that side of my brain had been too obvious about its interests, considering that Izmene said my teachers even noticed it. I try to wrack my brain on how they knew, and why I wasn't self-aware. I mean, Grey and Lara know all about it, of course they do, they're around me practically 24/7.

As the path winds closer to my house, I try to look for the silver lining of this whole situation. My curiosity of the old world had peaked Izmene's interest, and if I decide to take her offer, still very much to be determined, then I definitely won't have a boring job. But, on the other hand, maybe boring is better than hidden.

All too suddenly I realize I've started to walk right next to the tree-line again, the ground shifting to pine straw. Every fiber of my being wants to go see that shed, hear that music again, but if someone is there . . . I don't want to explain it. Don't want to be chased by anyone screaming at me to get off their property.

But . . .

There's a chance I could sit far enough away in order to stay out of view but also be able to hear the music. There's always a chance.

I take a step . . . another . . . another.

And then stop.

Someone else is walking.

I can hear the footsteps, small twigs breaking, and I freeze.

About thirty feet ahead, someone freezes as well, staring at me just as I'm staring at him.

I can't breathe. It's not the fact that I might potentially be in danger, but purely because I didn't expect anyone to be around. Especially no one my age. Even if someone did live in that shed, I don't think they would be on this side of the forest. But this person, it seems, perhaps had the same idea as I did.

"Hi."

I speak before I can even tell myself not to. Before I'm able to weigh the pros and cons.

That's never happened before. I've never not weighed the pros and cons of my decisions.

Fortunately, for me, the boy stares for a moment before continuing on, not responding to me in the slightest.

Good, I guess.

"A twenty! How the hell did you get a twenty?!" Grey exclaims.

"Work," I reply.

It has been two hours since I got home, and only thirty minutes since Grey and Lara appeared in my doorway. I haven't mentioned the boy in the forest, mostly because I don't think my friends would care. However, they might care about the fact that he's still there in the back of my mind. Shoulder-length dark hair, dark clothes, dark eyes. Walking the same way I was, perhaps even going to the shed, perhaps even listening to the same music that I wished to hear myself. That's when my friends would stop caring, at the fact that he's only occupying my brain because I love the thought of having someone else share my interests. The desire to know about the old world, to experience the good parts. That's when they would get bored. They understand, of course, but I don't think they would like to hear about it.

So, I don't mention it. There's no need.

Currently, it feels as if Grey is staring a rectangular-shaped hole straight through my hand. His gaze is relentless.

"The only work I know of where you can get a twenty is definitely not found in a library," Lara says as she holds out her hand and I reluctantly give her the card. She holds it up to inspect it under the light, even weighs it in her hand. "Huh, it's definitely real."

"Izmene is generous," I counter. I don't know why I just don't come out and tell them what I'd seen, what Izmene had revealed to me. But something stops me from sharing the truth.

"First name basis? I like it," Grey pats me on the shoulders.

Lara runs a hand through her hair, "We spend all day labeling random books in a hot ass room, and we don't get paid until next week."

"Alright, alright, let's leave her alone," Grey smiles, "but you're buying dinner for like three weeks, including today, let's go."

A part of me feels like I'm doing something wrong. I don't like keeping things from Grey and Lara. I could tell Lara, she's good at keeping secrets; Grey, on the other hand, is a different story. He doesn't do it on purpose, he just speaks extremely quickly without thinking. Call it a lack of filter, if you will.

"Where do you wanna go, Ira?" Grey asks, "Since dinner is on you, you get to pick."

He acts as if he's giving me some sort of present, something I should be overjoyed about, but he knows how I feel about decisions, especially with food. I can't do it.

"Funny, Grey, truly. We're going to Fern's," Lara moves to grab a black jacket from my closet before leaving my room, not waiting for either of us.

"Well, in my defense, I did want you to be able to choose."

I shake my head, "I like Fern's."

And I do, even more because I didn't have to be the one to choose.

"Should I keep the jacket?" Grey asks, observing himself in my mirror.

He looks good, and he knows it, so I assume he's asking because it might be a bit over the top for a place like Fern's, where you could probably walk in with a swimsuit on and they would still seat you. Mostly because, like many of the places in the area, the main patrons are students, coming in after sports practices or any other activities.

"I like it," my voice comes across with only half of the volume intended. Grey swings back towards me.

"You okay?"

"Yeah, just tired," I reach for a hair tie and pull my hair into a low ponytail, "Are you ready?"

It wasn't a lie, and it wasn't exactly the truth. I don't know what you would call it.

Fern's is only a five-minute walk from my house, three minutes at Lara's pace. It's a small building with sides of stainless steel and a front made of glass, potted plants scaling half of its length. Most of the architecture around here looks like this, especially in the city. Glass, steel, the occasional light grey concrete, and plants. So many plants. According to old accounts, Chapel Hill used to be mainly brick, but all of it was renovated years before the fall. When someone mentions a town made of brick nowadays, people tend to think of the older buildings in Apex, the ones still standing fifty years later with memorials for the people lost in the fall.

Outside, there's an array of wide metal pieces bent in odd shapes which from first glance, might look like an art exhibition. But, on second glance, you would realize that they're table and chairs, and oddly comfortable if I might add. The inside in extremely cozy, in one corner, a fireplace provides the majority of light along with the large windows. In another, a wall painted like a mountain scape separates the main room from the kitchen. The bar sits next to it, only holding about five people at a time, seven if some people stand, I guess. And, like the outside, plants. So many plants.

The three of us settle into the table closest to the fireplace. Even though there's a flock of students seated outside, in a wide range of different sport or work uniforms, the inside is rather empty. Two people are seated at the bar, talking nonstop, while there is only one other table filled with a family. Grey begins to talk about one of the books he noticed today at the library while Lara corrected him on every detail, but my mind was too clouded to focus, not that they needed me to anyway. I can't get Izmene out of my head, all of her words. *How did she know I knew what vinyl is? How do I know what vinyl is?*

Eventually, a young waiter came and took our order. I got spaghetti, like always, while Grey and Lara decided to share a steak. Every time we go out to eat at a place that doesn't happen to be Fern's, they gush about the steak here and how nothing compares. Personally, although the majority doesn't agree, I hate the taste of meat. I can handle it occasionally, like hot dogs for example, if you consider that meat. Sometimes I can even do chicken if it has enough breading around it to the point where it no longer tastes like meat. My friends have tried and tried to change this, all to no avail, almost as if it was a personal attack on them that I don't like meat. Fortunately, they eventually gave up.

"The cover did not have a naked man on it, Grey, you were seeing what you wanted to see," Lara takes a sip from her lemonade.

No idea what they're talking about, I completely zoned out.

"Oh, and you wouldn't read it if you had access to it?" asks Grey.

Her gaze slips towards the door behind me, "I never said that."

I hear the bells jangle above the doorframe as someone enters, the hair on my arms standing up as the cold night air enters, despite the warmth of the fireplace.

"You know," Grey lowers his voice, "the cover looked just like him."

Luckily enough for me, I don't even have to turn around.

The man—well, boy really, as he looks more like our age, strides to a table in front of us. If he really did look like the cover that

Grey noticed, I could see why he remembered it. The majority of his face is hidden by a shadow of absent firelight, but his mouth is firmly set in a small frown against his pale skin and sharp jawline, dark brown hair falling to his shoulders. From what I can tell, his eyes are dark, focusing on something in his hands. He's wearing a black turtleneck with a blazer over it of the same color, and a silver necklace hangs from his neck, but I can't make out what the charm is on the end of it.

He doesn't look real.

I try to focus back on the conversation, focusing my eyes on anything except for him. Except for the fact that I've seen him before.

The boy from the forest.

The one that was walking towards the shed, just like I was.

And now he's here, just like I am.

Grey catches my attention shifting and asks if I need to get some sleep, and though that does seem nice at the moment, I don't think I can move. I'm rooted in place.

In my school's library, there's a small section dedicated to magazines from before the fall. It's honestly surprising we even have it in the first place, but Petrichor stated sections like it were kept in order for students to understand what types of dangerous thinking led to the eventual fall. I assume they mean the political disagreements and what not, but typically, those were the parts the students ignored, including myself. There was one magazine from 1995, in which a section of it detailed "the heartthrobs of the decade so far," including musicians and actors. I only flipped through it briefly once, but from what I remember, I think the figure across from us could have been a contender. Now that I think about it, maybe I heard about vinyl through these magazines.

I try to wrack my brain, but I can't remember any article at all that even mentioned the word.

However, the magazines are truly not the reason my gaze keeps slipping back to him, it's because of the way he's acting. Suspicious, maybe? Nervous? It's hard to tell what; I won't let myself fully look at him. I don't know what it is, but something seems off. I can't mention it to Grey or Lara because they'll either be creeped out and make us get out of there, which might be the better option, or they'll turn towards him and make everything uncomfortably obvious. Honestly, I don't want either of those options.

I know I'm right when I finally give in and glance at him, and he's staring right back. Staring *through* me. I know I'm just imagining it, but his eyes stare like he knows every regret and mistake I've ever made. Like he can't move his eyes away from my own.

"How long until the food is here?" I swallow, taking a sip of my water.

Grey leans towards me, "Do you wanna leave and mess around with that guy in the back alley?"

Lara kicks him under the table.

"Because if you won't, then I will-" Grey chimes in.

If I was in a better mood, and not slightly scared, I might have laughed, maybe even have told Grey he should go over and ask him out. But, at the moment, words fail me.

Our waiter comes back out of the kitchen, setting two take out containers on the table in front of the mystery man and asking him to wait just a moment for him to grab his check. The second the waiter leaves, he stands and moves quickly to the door.

Before either of us can stop him, Grey brings him to a halt by practically yelling, "You're dressed way too fucking nicely to not be able to pay for that!"

When he turns, I see his face fully. Our age. Brown eyes.

"I stole the clothes too" He retorts.

And he's out the door, disappearing as he turns the corner.

"I'm not dealing with it!" I hear the waiter complain when he comes back out, "I'll call the Thieves Defend on my break."

I don't blame him. I'm surprised Grey didn't practically run after him, but he's usually more bark than bite.

"He sounded like he hasn't talked in days," Lara whispers.

She's right. His voice was low and raspy, like what someone sounds like when they're still getting over a major cold. He was grinning when he said it.

"He sounded like a fucking asshole," Grey shrugs, smiling sweetly as the waiter grabs his empty glass.

It's been a couple hours since Fern's. The rest of dinner was fine, the spaghetti was good, but all I could think about was going home, which eventually, we did. Somehow, they always end up at my house. I don't know why, but we've all subconsciously chosen my room to be our place to meet.

"Well, I'm gonna head out," Lara whistles quietly. "Are you good for tonight, Grey?"

He does a mock salute. Even though I would appreciate some alone time to process what happened at both the library and Fern's, I can't help but be confused.

"What's—" before I can finish, she's already out the door.

I flip over on my bed to face Grey. His back is turned towards me, braiding his hair between his fingers. His hair mixes with his skin tone nicely; I've never noticed that before.

"Where are you going tonight?" I ask.

He pauses.

"My lips are sealed."

I frown. "Grey, you can't do that. You know you can tell me things, even if Lara says you shouldn't."

He turns around, "How did you know she told me not to?"

"She's the only one you listen to," I smile.

Grey scoffs and repeats my reply in a mocking voice, "That's not true, I listen to you."

"Barely, but that's because I don't tell you what to do nearly as much."

"Fair point . . . anyways, we're going to a meeting which I'm quite excited about because . . ."

His tongue rattles off as quickly as ever. He reclines slowly next to me, foreseeing his death by Lara's hands.

"What kind of meeting?"

"Do you really want me to die? I thought you cared about me." He starts to fake cry. He's perfected it by now.

"Curiosity killed . . . well, you, I guess."

Grey takes one of my pillows and screams into it.

"Fine, fine, *god*, it's a Petrichor meeting."

My eyes squint, trying to make sense of what he just said. The person who dislikes Petrichor . . . is going to one of their meetings? How did he even get into it? I mean, Grey is eighteen, technically an adult . . . however odd that is to imagine.

He begins to laugh, "I can nearly hear your thoughts, you know, so I'm gonna rephrase. It's a 'we-don't-exactly-trust-Petrichor' meeting."

Yeah, I think to myself, nodding my head.

That makes more sense.

"Why bring it up at all if Lara didn't want me to know about it? I mean, she didn't bring it up directly, but must've known I'd ask you about it."

Grey makes a sound, thinking, "After she told me not to mention it to you, I tried to convince her that she can talk about it. Maybe that was her trying, even though she left the hard work for me."

I open my mouth to reply before he stops me, "Questions, I know, questions. This is our first time going. Some people came up to us in the library today, obviously eavesdropping on the conversation Lara and I were having. They invited us to the meeting; it's at the park rather late tonight. I don't think Lara meant any harm by not wishing to tell you, she just didn't want you to think that we're like, well, working against your family or anything."

The park. I haven't been to the park in forever. I want to ask more questions about the meeting, but my mind goes foggy.

My eyes trace the pictures on my wall as Grey falls silent. I can feel him watching me, but I don't mind. My brain ignites sometimes like this when I find a topic I haven't thought about recently. I don't exactly know what I do outwardly that makes it obvious but Grey always notices. And he never interrupts. Just watches. Observes as my mind retraces past steps.

God, it's beautiful. This might sound ridiculous, apologies, but it's true. It feels less like a park and more like a valley that goes on for miles. The ground is completely covered in clovers and small white flowers. Trees dot the landscape like they were flicked on by a paintbrush. There's one tree in particular, not sure the name of it, that I'm absolutely attached to. Always have been, not sure why. It would be the perfect place to lie under, feel the breeze, contemplate whatever it is you need to contemplate—the world, maybe? Or life.

"Ira . . . hey, I gotta go, okay?" Grey's voice brings me back.

I quickly open my eyes; I didn't even realize that I had dozed off.

"I'm sorry, Grey," I yawn.

He rests his hands on the sides of my face, eyes kind, "Don't worry about it, you needed to sleep. I have to go to that thing now." He pauses before adding, "You know you can come if you want. I doubt people would mind."

"It's okay, Lara would probably be uncomfortable with me being there."

He shakes my head between his hands. He shows affection in his own way.

But he doesn't try to disagree with me either. Grey knows just as much as I do how Lara would feel if I was there.

"I love you, Ira."

"I love you too, Grey."

Chapter Five

March 24, 2073

12:00 PM

Does that make sense?" Izmene asks, casting me a look that screams she doesn't want to explain it again.

Luckily, considering how simple this task seems, she shouldn't have to. All I'm doing is taking crates, removing the stickers from the vinyl that Izmene attached, adding different vinyl into each crate and putting stickers on those.

Fun.

It's been a couple of days since Grey and Lara went to that meeting. I was told it went well.

Lara barely talked about it.

I hope Grey will explain later.

But who knows?

Going back to the library today was odd, Izmene seemed different, paranoid maybe. I tried to distract myself by memorizing some of the album names and artists, but only one really stuck in my head. Four men lay on the ground, their heads only inches apart. A lot of purples, blues, and yellows. CALM is the name of the album. Which is, ironically, the exact opposite of what I feel at the moment. I saw my friends this morning but they seemed odd, just like Izmene, like their brains were off on a different planet. Maybe they're tired, I don't know. Maybe I'm overreacting. Part of me wishes I went to the meeting with them, just so that I wouldn't feel almost like an outsider. Lara wouldn't have liked it, I know, but maybe if I would've explained myself, she would have understood. I think Grey understands, as much as he can. Or maybe he's just saying what he thinks I need to hear to make me feel better.

Before I can stop myself, I apologize to Izmene and ask if I can walk outside for a bit to get some fresh air.

"You don't have to apologize, you know that," she smiles, "you can go out the back door if you wish to avoid other people."

Good idea.

I walk as quickly as possible towards the back door, keeping my head low. The last thing I want at the moment is a conversation. With anyone, quite honestly. Opening the door, I prepare myself to be greeted with the crisp midday air.

Instead, I stop in my tracks.

The man, boy, guy, thief, whatever, from Fern's stands in front of me, his eyes calm.

He's holding a crate.

"Are you stalking me?" He asks.

It takes me a moment to process everything, "what?"

"I asked you a question."

There are a multitude of different ways he could have said that to not sound like a dick.

"No, I'm not stalking you, why—I work here."

He stares at me.

Today he's wearing a black t-shirt, cut just above his hipbones, with pants of the same color riding just below.

Wow.

"Well, I'll be taking these." He says before turning and walking back towards the tree line.

"Wait," I gather myself, "are they yours? Are you supposed to-"

"Izmene gave them to me angel, calm yourself." He calls back.

And he's gone.

I rush back inside, ignoring the way he spoke and acted and the way I feel—it doesn't matter. It doesn't matter that when I look at him, I feel the same way I do when I look at Izmene. Almost like I'm comforted but confused at the same time. I don't even know how to explain it, not even to myself. I haven't really noticed it until today, especially after seeing both Izmene and him in practically the same minute.

"Izmene, a boy just took a crate from out back, was he supposed to or should I call the Thieves Defend?"

Her eyes go wide, "he came here now? Outside?"

I nod, it takes her a moment to compose herself.

"They're his. I was going to deliver them but I guess he's fine coming to grab them now."

She's surprised, and I want more than anything to ask more questions, but I can't tell if it's a touchy subject or not.

"You saw him?" Izmene asks, analyzing me.

I nod again, I didn't know we were delivering them to people my age, I thought-

"You know what, Meira, it's been a long day. Take this," she hands me another twenty, "I think you can go home early."

This feels wrong.

"Are you sure?" I protest, "I'm fine staying and finishing."

She shakes her head and practically pushes me out of the vinyl room, "I promise, now go."

It doesn't really seem like I have many other options.

Walking home, I try to figure out what the hell just happened. Obviously, somehow Izmene and this kid know each other. I don't think he works for her, only because if he did, he would know who I am if we both worked for the same person doing the same thing. She's never spoken about family, granted I've only known her a couple days, but that's not what this seems like. My only logical guess is that maybe he has a parent or grandparent from before the fall that Izmene delivers records to, and he decided to grab them himself today. But why did she act so confused, so nervous about me leaving?

Maybe I can ask her in a couple days when it seems as if her paranoia has slowed.

A small part of me is almost glad that these weird occurrences keep happening, they keep my mind off of my friends and family. Friends who seem distant and family that is physically distant. A work trip, currently.

But, when I finally get home, there's absolutely no distractions.

I look at my eyes in the mirror as deeply as possible. They feel almost foreign today, somehow saddened and dull. I wonder if they look at me the same way I look at them? I sigh, running a finger along the edge of my collarbone. I have the whole house to myself; my parents are working . . . my friends are working . . . and now it's just me. I can do whatever I want, but my brain carries me to my bed. I curl up into a tight shell and stare at the small folds of the blanket. My eyes shift around my room and land on the desk, specifically to a small plastic bag.

Interesting.

I have no idea how it got there; I assume my parents left it. A mystery, or an accident. Standing, I slowly make my way over and pick it up. There's nothing in it or under it, just a clear plastic bag. I make a mental note to ask my parents about it later, or never if I forget.

I nestle myself under the pillow until I can no longer hear the crickets outside. The inevitability of my emotions is bound to come, so why not let it happen?

A lonely tear runs down my cheek. Others tears follow, not wanting to be left behind.

I get this feeling of peace sometimes. You know, usually, when people hold in emotions for too long, they explode. That's the normal thing to do. That's what everyone does. But, when it gets too much for me, I feel at peace. I *become* peace. I am peace. You would assume that's a good thing, something everyone would want, right? Well, it's the worst feeling I've ever experienced. See, when a person is at peace, people assume it's either because they're dead or they're extremely happy. However, there's an in-between that everyone misses. I become at peace because I can no longer function. I shut down. All of my emotions join hands and dance circles around my mind until they go so fast, they finally form fog. They laugh and they cry and they look at the damage they caused to my brain and go, "Wow, who knew we could do this?" And to that, I say, "You knew . . . you all knew. Yet you did it anyway." Eventually, they stop one by one. Problems get solved, but they're always there in the background. They like to play hide and seek, it's their favorite game. Happiness is always the seeker. Always trying to stay in the know, until it doesn't. Until the other emotions come out of the dark and rip happiness to shreds; then I start all over again.

I don't like when I get in this mood. I hate it, to be honest, and I don't really hate a lot of things. Everyone sees me happy, and that's how I prefer it. I like helping people. I don't want to sound like I believe myself to be a saint or anything, because I'm not, but my friends being happy makes me happy. It's always been like that. It's never bothered me, and that's okay. That mindset would be good for some people, people who can have a good balance of helping others and helping themselves.

See, I don't exactly have that balance. To my parents, humanity is good. Humanity should be helped. I should help humanity. They never said that directly but that's what I got out of it. I don't think they really meant to have this exact effect; this effect, being that I don't exactly know how to help myself. My emotions are hidden, even from myself; very rarely do they come out. Like right now, for example. I make sure to never show it in front of people, and it works. Sometimes people take advantage of the way my mind works, whether it be for money, food, etc. I don't usually mind, but even if I did, I couldn't exactly do anything about it. I don't really know how to talk back to people, how to stick up for myself. Never had an instance where I had to. There were probably times where I should have, but it always worked out in the long run. I try to imag-ine what the other person is going through, everyone has problems. I just hope that eventually they'll get over it and stop treating other people differently because of it.

I smash my face into the pillow and sigh. I don't even know what happened today. It's gotten worse, recently. I don't know if it's because school is out and that's one more distraction down the drain, or if it's purely just bad timing. I've felt it begin to bubble this past week, sped along by whatever feeling I get when I encounter Izmene and . . . whoever he is. A mystery. Maybe that's what I'll call him from now on, Mystery.

But, finding the cause for these feelings won't change anything. I want to get out of this. I need to get out of this. Maybe the mirror will help, to see myself, to ground myself. One step . . . good, now another . . . why is this so hard right now? My body feels like it wants to crumble. Why is my arm so sore? I haven't been eating a lot recently. I don't mean to; I just don't have an appetite. Maybe people are right, maybe I do look unhealthy. Maybe that's why my body feels like it could snap under the weight of a heavier-than-usual coat. I did it, though. I made it to the mirror. When I look at my body, I understand why sometimes I get concerned comments on my appearance. I don't look good. When the world switched, so did beauty standards; by switch I mean they disappeared. Extremely thankful for it, too. The thing about these standards was that they were fully society-driven. When the extinction of said society is threatened, these standards are not the main focus. Petrichor took their time to keep them as mere mistakes of the past, which is exactly what they are. It took some time for the older generations to get used to this but eventually, they succumbed. My parents went to school after Petrichor had already taken over, and they learned about all of the mistakes our past society made just like I did. Even without these standards, I still look unnatural, health-wise.

I run my hands through my hair. It's long now, especially on the days where I straighten it. The same color as dirt, Grey likes to say. He's joking, but it's true. My eyes reflect my hair color almost perfectly, so one could say that they're dirt too. I've accepted it.

When I get in this state, an overwhelming sense of guilt always comes with it. Last time, it was when I thought Grey and Lara hated me for a joke I made during lunch. I was wrong of course, but this, as well as the stress of school in general, had me drowning just like now. Sometimes the guilt comes in different forms, today it's based upon the fact that I feel like I should be doing something, that I should be a part of something. I mean, hell, some girls my age before the fall were already famous musicians or helping scientists find cures for incurable diseases . . . I don't know. My friends are joining groups and finding their own things to be a part of. But I just sit here. I'm thankful for the position that I've been put in and everything in my life, you can trust me on that, but I feel like I need to pay it back in some way. Do good. Somehow.

However, I guess the most important thing at this moment would be to distract myself until Lara and Grey get here, until I do figure out something to be a part of. Because, inevitably, they always come straight back here.

Chapter Six

March 26, 2073

1:00 PM

You have to be kidding me.

I was not mentally prepared to be immediately met with this, the second I walk out of the record room and into the main library.

The boy, mystery-man, or whatever is browsing one of the sections, and turns directly towards me, meaning that I can't even try to avoid his gaze.

"So, you are a stalker." He says.

I inhale.

Exhale.

"I work here, I think I told you that last time."

He nods, "I thought it was a rather rigorous process to get a position here, no? What made you so special?"

The way his dark green sweater makes it seem as if he was made to walk these shelves has me suddenly forgetting why I walked out here in the first place.

Focus.

"They didn't tell me."

"So, there's a chance you were a candidate out of desperation?"

What?

Why—I can't control my frustration beginning to boil at his suggestion.

"You think they chose me because they had no other option?"

"I'm not talking about whoever *they* are, I'm talking about Izmene. Why she chose you to work for her specifically?" He moves a step closer, "You don't seem to have any outstanding qualities that would make you different from the rest, but feel free to refute me if you feel so inclined."

"I'm sorry, do you even know me? How did you know—"

"Meira! Were you looking for me? I apologize."

Izmene's voice is the only buffer between me and my confusion. I have seen this boy multiple random times, have barely spoken a word to him, and now he's acting as if he knows all about me. Making suggestions that I shouldn't be here, that I don't deserve to be here?

What the actual hell?

I am not a person that angers easily, I barely even know what it feels like to be mad, but now it feels like it's inevitable. Just purely based on the fact he doesn't know me and already assumed that I didn't—

"Meira?"

"I—yes, sorry, I was looking for you."

Izmene nods, glancing at the boy, "did you need something?"

'No," his eyes burn a hole in my soul, "I was just leaving."

Izmene shuts the door behind us as we enter into the record room, my blood still at a slight simmer.

"Did he . . . say something? You seem . . . I'm not sure." Izmene inquires.

Inhale.

Exhale.

"I'm just confused. He was asking me how I got the job here, how I was the only one that was chosen by you."

She takes a moment to consider, stacking loose records in a crate as she does so, "He's here a lot, and an asshole every time."

I try my best not to laugh. This was the first time I've heard her curse.

It's refreshing, in a way.

"So, are the records he took last time for himself, or for someone in his family?"

Izmene shakes her head, "I assume for himself, I don't ask questions. The only reason he knows about this in the first place was that he was also a candidate for this position. You and him share a common interest in the old world, though I assume his might be a bit different."

"What do you mean?"

Based on my opinion of him so far, I can only guess that he holds interests of the old world for all of the wrong reasons. All of the reasons it ended in the first place.

He just seems like the type.

"I just doubt he holds many of the warm sentiments that you do."

Exactly.

Izmene shrugs once before handing me another stack of stickers in the shape of red circles.

I study them, "I've never seen these before."

"Put them on the records in that corner," she points to the opposite side of the room, "the red circle means that family, or person, or whatnot is in a dire situation. The music helps, in one way or another."

By the time she finished, her skin has grown pale.

At this point, I don't wish to know what qualifies as a dire situation.

Once back home, Lara and Grey flop onto my bed before I jump out of the way. Almost. I can see sweat filtering through Grey's white shirt; they didn't dress up this time. No one really cares what other people wear anymore to be honest, but it can still make a good or bad first impression for work. I guess they're past the need to make a further impression.

"Was it that hot in the main rooms today?"

I pause, realizing that I had misspoken. As far as they knew, I was working in the main library as well. Hence, same temperature.

"Pretty sure you were in the same library we were," Grey whispers, half of his face hidden by his jacket.

"Maybe it's because you wear that jacket almost every day," says Lara as she takes one of my pillows to hit the back of his head. No reason, I assume.

Grey groans, "Leave me and my jacket alone."

They continue to bicker, fully forgetting about my comment—unless they never caught on—which is good. Maybe I shouldn't lie to them. I mean, what's the worst that could happen? A lot. Actually. Not that I personally believe Petrichor to be a true threat to Izmene's operation, she obviously has some sort of reason to be as paranoid as she is. Because of that, I can assume there's something else she's hiding from, someone else, maybe? But either way, I don't want to lose my job either, if she ever figured out I told them.

"Oh Romeo, where are you, Romeo?" Grey swoons dramatically across Lara's shoulders.

I quickly turn to face him, "Not even close to the actual quote."

"There she is. You really are quite easy. Your attention, I mean."

"It works every time," Lara joins in. "Especially with, what's the title, *hopeless romantics?*"

I hope she never says that again.

Without my response, she wraps her arms around me in an attempt to pull me to their level. She's still chuckling almost silently as I give in and settle between them. Laying here, staring at the ceiling, is a common occurrence for us.

Tradition.

"Any advice for tonight?" asks Grey.

Ah. He's is talking about his date. *First* date. "I was just labeled a hopeless romantic and now you're asking for advice?"

Lara lifts her hands in surrender, "I'm out of this. Also, you being a romantic more than qualifies you for this."

I exhale, "A romantic with slim to no experience."

"Grey has enough experience for the three of us combined."

He scrunches his nose before throwing a blanket over Lara's head, "Shhh, go to sleep. Sleepy time."

"What's their name again?"

Grey starts to smile from ear to ear, "Their name is Cora and they are perfect in every way, shape, and form. Just saying their name feels like an honor."

I match his grin; it was hard not to after that description. He doesn't really have the best reputation for long-term relationships, but he's never described anyone like that. It was always, "yeah she's really nice" or "he's tall and surprisingly not a douchebag" and so on. God, I hope he falls in love. Actually, let me rephrase. I hope he falls in love with a person who can *reciprocate* it. I've always loved that word, reciprocate. I've only used it twice. Well, meaning that my feelings have only been reciprocated twice. One time when I was really young; we decided to stay friends. The second time was two years ago; we just weren't right for each other. I've fallen in love multiple times, hence the name hopeless romantic. People probably think I'm lying, now that I think about it. Meira, how have you fallen in love four times in the span of 16 years? Wish I knew. Wish I didn't. Well, it felt good at the moment, not so much afterward, obviously. Having a crush would be too simple. In almost every instance of a crush, it almost always evolved into love. It wasn't true love, but it was love nonetheless. When I grew to love someone, I wanted to help them. I wanted to help their emotions until they were happy; downside is I didn't give a shit about my own emotions. They were unimportant. This happened four times. Each time I would never act on my emotions, meaning I would never tell them how I felt or anything like that, and each time they ended up leaving. It was an endless cycle of me falling in love, not acting on it fully, them leaving, and me being broken. Messy, I guess. However, I do know how I want to be treated. I told myself I wouldn't fall for anyone else for a while. It's been two years, so I've stuck with it. Maybe I'm ready now, who knows. But, either way, there are more pressing matters to attend to. "What if they don't like breadsticks?"

"Grey, what?" Lara asks, sticking her head out of the blanket.

"It's a good question."

"Get them a necklace."

He mentioned that Cora likes jewelry, so we'll start there.

"I already did, and a bracelet, and two rings. Shit, what if they're ugly?" He reaches into his pocket to dump a mound of silver on my bed, "See if they're ugly."

I reach my hand over to try and untangle the mess of chains. The longer I do it the more it seems impossible.

"Pretty hard to tell what they look like."

"Lara, I love you. I really do, but please tone down the commentary for like two seconds."

She rolls her eyes as Grey continues to try and help me tame the wild beast of jewelry.

"I shouldn't have put them in my pocket."

I nod, "exactly."

"This seems like a lot more than four pieces of jewelry," Lara whispers, I assume in an attempt to try and contain the comments that are fighting to spew themselves from her mouth.

I might be wrong, but I swear Grey starts to blush. I've never seen him do that.

"I just want Cora to be happy."

"They will be. They would be happy even without the gifts."

He seems to calm down after I say that, making the little people-pleaser in my brain finally quiet down.

"Well, since you have a hot date tonight, I think Meira and I should go on one of our own," Lara states, taking my hand as she stands from the bed. "I can't promise an answer, but message us if needed."

I already know what this is.

And I'm not thrilled.

But, even if I'm not exactly happy about it, it is finally a distraction.

"We're gonna see someone we know," I whisper, huddling as close to Lara as possible. It wasn't a question, more of a statement that I know to be true. We always seem to run into people we know, or more so people that Grey and Lara know.

Despite the fact that it's a warmer night, a slight chill has seeped its way into my skin.

"Keep your head down then, princess," She whispers back.

We had decided to go to Paul's. Well, by *we* I mean Lara decided. However, I probably should have given my opinion about this one. Paul's is located in Chapel Hill, so it took a very short bus ride to make our way here. It has two owners; Paul, obviously, who's the head chef of the restaurant, and his husband Luke who is the DJ for the club portion. The outside of the building is almost split in half, the left side being the restaurant. In front, there's a small patio with out-door seating and a fireplace where the waiters will bring drinks and usually what they're best known for, pizza. The inside of the restaurant portion is smaller, quite similar to Fern's except for a bit more crowded. The other side, however, is almost the complete opposite. A large room, meant only for partying and drinking, packed full.

Of course, since it's extremely popular and relatively close to my school, I can confidently say that every student comes here at least once a week, but I don't blame them. Even as I try to keep my eyes glued to the floor, things keep catching my attention as we make our way to the club section. The artificial stars twinkling above us, lightly matching the beat of the song coming from the next room. The music takes us where we need to go, luckily, so I don't even have to look up.

The shift in the air is immediate and almost unbearable as we cross the archway that separates the main restaurant from the dance hall. So much for the breeze, it's like a sauna in here. I close my eyes and sigh. Part of me had hoped that for once it wouldn't be crowded but, obviously, I am wrong. A lot of dancing bodies equals heat, which inevitably explains the temperature of the room. And, lo and behold, I am right. Lara is already on the dance floor by the time I tilt my eyes forward. She's always confident but nothing compares to the way she acts when she dances. I've asked her before why she's so good, especially with never even having lessons; Lara explained that, to her, it's not dancing, it's a feeling. Whatever that means. Music is like a distant cousin to me. I don't know it very well, but part of me wants to. Part of me feels like I need to, hence my interest in vinyl and the music from the shed in the woods.

The shed.

I feel like I've barely thought about it since Grey took me near it, but at the same time, like it has always been in the back of my mind. Lurking, waiting for the perfect moment to grab my full attention.

But, at the moment, I can't focus on anything except for Lara.

To be honest, I don't understand how she feels anything from this. There doesn't seem to be any real effort, or maybe even work, put into these songs. Sometimes they don't even have words. I love the songs I hear in the movies they show at school. They seem real; they have feelings. Maybe I don't quite understand how or why she loves *this* music, but I can admire how she manages to make something out of nothing.

"How is it?" I ask as I hand Lara a cup of water.

"Fucking hot as hell. You should come on the dance floor," She replies.

I shake my head, "I might, just not right now."

Lie.

"It's not gonna get less crowded, you know."

A smile escapes from my lips, "Then it looks like I'm staying."

"Are we going to have to have one of those moments?" Lara asks.

"Moments?" I reply.

"You know, where I have to drag you unwillingly to the dance floor," Lara laughs, still slightly moving her body with the music. She believes this to be an old teen drama.

"No, we're not."

"Come on, we have to move before Grey gets here."

She almost dislocates my shoulders, pulling me out of the chair and in-between two extremely tall people. Damn, why are they so tall? Why did Lara have to drag me to the most intimidating spot in the whole room? "What do you mean before Grey gets here?" I ask her, looking up at one of the tall figures in passing, making a mental note not to accidentally bump into one of them.

Her signature sly grin appears; never good.

We're spying on him. We're definitely spying on him.

"What are best friends good for if not to do shit like this?" She kisses the top of my hand.

I can't say no to her. I know sometimes it can be fun to be cliché, but not when it risks a friendship. I am likely overthinking this, but I can honestly see Grey ignoring Lara and I for about a week and a half for this.

You know, I could run away. I've never really heard of anyone doing it for real, but it always seems like a good solution to a problem, especially in movies. Maybe making impulsive decisions always leads to a good adventure. I wouldn't really know. This would be a good time to run away, I think. It's crowded enough in here that no one would really notice. Lara would obviously, but I think she would forgive me. Where would I go? It doesn't matter, I'm not going to do it, but if I was, maybe I would go back to the shed. It seems abandoned on the outside, most likely on the inside too besides the music. If there's a person actually living there then maybe they'll take me under their wing. Maybe they'll realize I want to be like them; away, unbothered, listening to actual music. But then again, maybe Grey is right. Maybe it was just some horny teenagers. Maybe it's their getaway just the same as I want it to be mine. Well, actually, it's different, obviously. A lot different. You know, I can see Izmene living there. Locked away with her books and her vinyl. I wonder if she's married. I wonder if I'm thinking way too much in a moment like this. I wonder if I really should be focusing on where Lara is guiding me. I wonder if Grey can see us considering he's about two feet away.

"Are you two serious?" Grey groans.

I wonder if running away was the best option.

Chapter Seven

March 26, 2073

8:00 PM

"You never told us you were coming here!" Lara whispers frantically to Grey.

I don't exactly know if that's what she said, but I can assume. When Grey caught us, the rage in his eyes was palpable. He doesn't seem too angry at me, thankfully, but Lara is a different story. They're arguing about ten feet away from us, Cora and I. He was right when he was describing them. They look ethereal. Their hair is similar to Izmene's, maybe even longer. I don't know what type of dye they used but I should really ask; it's silver, I think, but at a different angle, it almost looks white. The exact opposite of mine in both color and style. Cora is dressed like nothing I've ever seen. The outfit seems like it came straight from the past: a loose-fitting button down with flowing white pants. Retro, maybe, would be a good word—you don't hear it much anymore. Many people look at the past through a pessimistic lens; barely anyone wants to be associated with it anymore.

I don't exactly know what to say to Cora, if I even should, or how I would go about it.

Luckily, they beat me to it, "Personally, I think it's funny."

Their voice.

Beautiful.

It reminds me of the voice you hear in your head while trying to convince yourself that everything will be okay. Guiding, yet haunting.

"I think Grey wanted everything to be perfect tonight; he didn't plan on this part," I sigh.

Cora smiles gently, "It was perfect, I mean, it still is," they pause. "He said that he wanted me to meet you guys, and as it turns out, it just happened earlier than he had planned."

I turn to fully face them, "I really like your outfit."

They smile brighter now, meeting my eyes. Weird. Their eyes invoke the same feeling that Izmene's do. It's like an electric current shooting through me, one that draws my focus away from anything else. It's not a bad shock, but a shock nonetheless. A new shock, with the feeling of old.

"Meira." Their voice switches to a concerned tone.

I blink, trying to recognize whether or not I'm seeing things or if their face matches the exact one I have. Do they have the same feeling I do?

They shake their head and take a step forward, "It's Meira, right? Or do you like being called Ira?"

I recall how Izmene asked the same thing. "Either one," I try to attempt a smile.

They tilt their head towards the others, "Are they going to be okay?"

"They will be, I think. Grey's hands are relaxed . . . he's not angry."

"His hands change when he's upset?"

I look down, "He makes fists. He has a temper, which isn't always a bad thing. He would never hit anyone, but he has broken a couple of walls."

"Seems sort of like a bad temper to me," Cora whispers.

I bite my tongue. I definitely shouldn't have said that.

"He's strong-willed is all. So is Lara, which is why they collide. Both of their tempers won't back down."

Cora immediately seems to lighten as we both exhale.

"So we can stay?" I ask, fully wanting the answer to be yes, despite being at Paul's. I like Cora, a lot. They're interesting to me. I don't find a lot of people like that.

Grey shifts his feet, "We can one hundred percent kick both of them out, Cora. There are no consequences."

Maybe.

They shake their head, "Let them stay."

I try to count the seconds between Cora's answer and Lara dragging them away to dance . . . it was four. That's how she does introductions, less awkward if I were to guess. I feel like Lara can almost completely guess a person's personality just based on how they dance. She's never been in a relationship before, nor does she want to be, but all I know is that if she had a partner, they would have to be an incredible dancer.

"How has it been so far?" I ask Grey, hoping to distract him before he remembers his anger.

It doesn't work.

He glares at me, "It was perfect. You know, it was like a fairy tale."

I'll try it again, "We talked while you and Lara were whispering."

"About what?"

I have prevailed, he's distracted.

"They like you," I smile.

Grey blushes, again, turning his head towards the dance floor.

His eyes filter through the crowd, searching. I watch his face closely as his eyes land upon Cora. There's almost an immediate switch in his eyes. I had never seen them look like that: infatuated.

The rest of the night was a blur. We talked for hours, mostly about Cora. They're not self-centered, but confident enough to enjoy answering questions. It's an impressive quality to have. I wish I did.

From what I've gathered, Cora helps out some days in the library, which is where they met Grey. They love plants. They love computers. When Lara asked them about where they went to school, Cora changed the subject.

At some point, I completely lost the topic of conversation. Grey's arm is around Cora now, lightly stroking their arm with his thumb. "He cried about it for days," Lara laughs, twirling a straw around her drink.

She persuaded the bartender that she was twenty-two, so she said. Though, while she was dancing, I tried a sip . . . it's only lemonade.

"I should have done a lot more than cry," Grey responds. "Lara should have been six feet under. Would have been if not for my divine forgiveness."

The table laughs as I try to match the energy. I don't even know what story they're telling. I've begun to feel like I shouldn't be here. Even though my parents said they were not going to return until morning, sometimes plans change. People can call me a rule-follower, goodie-two-shoes, but I'd rather not get in trouble. I never really have before. My parents trust me, and I'd like to keep it that way. Besides, I'm having a harder and harder time dialing into the conversation.

"Hey, I'm really sorry, but I think I'm going to head out," I say quietly, slowly standing up from my seat.

Chapter 7

There is instant disapproval. I didn't hear what was said specifically, but I can assume. Lara huffs and turns her head away from me, as is common whenever I get into this mood. It's a joke, even though sometimes it scares me.

Cora stands up to hug me, making eye contact for a second too long. Are they trying to tell me something? I can't read signals very well. For now, I'll choose not to worry about it.

After using the 'I'm really tired' excuse about five times, I finally head out the door. The breeze feels nice, like the cool side of a pillow. I tend to get cold extremely easily, but tonight is different. Tonight seems to match my body temperature perfectly. Tonight, outside, away from everything, it's perfect.

Well, maybe not.

You know, maybe being a rule follower isn't the best thing. What if they're talking about me? At the same time though, why would they? Questions start to spiral through my head as I switch my glance between the sky and the road ahead. The stars look indescribable. They always do. I've seen stars in the old movies, they never looked like these. The stars that I know are pleased with what they watch. Whenever my mom sees pictures of the past stars, she calls them dead. They weren't, but they looked like they wanted to be.

"You're going the wrong way, you know," a voice behind me says.

My heart begins to beat faster until it almost feels dangerous. I barely even realized that I was walking towards the abandoned shed and not home. The second I heard the voice, I could feel the blood rush from my face, my stomach dropping until it has nowhere else to go. My head feels like it's going to split in half, divided by an axe that's being held by whoever's behind me.

My mind screams at me to move but my body stays put.

"Home is to the left. This isn't left," the voice whispers. I spin around, praying this is a joke. Maybe a dream. The pain in my head begins to turn blinding.

Suddenly, I feel a sharp pinch in my shoulder.

If this is a dream, I hope to wake up to the same stars.

Chapter Eight

March 27, 2073

6:00 PM

"How do you know when love is real? Would you even know if it was fake?

I've never known the answer.

I can barely tell when I'm in love until months later, when I close my eyes and see theirs staring back at me. If someone said they loved me, would I truly be able to look in their eyes and know? I don't even know if I love myself. Must someone love themself before someone else?

When I look into Grey's eyes, I see love. A platonic love, but love nonetheless. I wonder sometimes if the old movies and books have fooled me into believing something false. Have they cursed me to set unrealistic expectations that will never be filled? All I know is I saw how Grey looked at Cora. He loves them. But how did he know? How could he be certain, and so quickly, too? Was it a conscious choice?"

I sigh, breathing in the cool night air, realizing that I'm not going to get my answers by talking to a dog.

The creature whines.

"That's not very helpful. Do you have anything that can help me?"

This time, when the dog whines once more, it drops a syringe onto the forest floor.

I pick it up, studying the swirling brown liquid within, the bubbles moving with it.

When I look back at the dog, it was no longer a wriggling creature, but a human figure. I wasn't frightened, nor was I surprised.

I felt comforted.

"It will help."

Gazing into the figure's eyes, I am met with all of the answers to any of my questions. It looked at me like I was its reason for living. For death. Like I was its water, its fire, its air. I was everything it would ever need. I was its darkness. I was its light.

I was its pleasure and its pain.

I felt happier than I ever had before. I was safe. I was where I was meant to be.

And then it was gone.

Before I could stop myself, I jammed the needle of the syringe into my eye.

One, and then the other.

I woke up to a cool liquid running down my face, pooling into a puddle under my chin. The pain in my head doesn't allow me to open my eyes at first, but I don't feel as if I need to. I feel safe. I'm somewhere, in a room, next to—

I jolt, forcing my eyes to peel open. I thought I knew where I was, I swore I was—I don't know where but it wasn't here. Not in my own room. I was . . . I don't know where.

Swallowing, I look down to see blood slowly running down the front of my shirt.

Chapter 8

"*Shit,*" I whisper, frantically making my way over to the mirror. It's my nose. It's just my nose. A nosebleed.

I exhale.

Just a nosebleed.

I've never had a nosebleed before.

Grabbing a towel from my closet, I hold it under my nose while I turn on my shower and yank the bloody clothes off.

Is there a way to stop nosebleeds? I assume it's this, I mean, how else would you do it? When the shower is finally hot enough, I discard the towel and let the blood drain with the swirling water. The sight reminds me of my dream.

The dream.

What the hell was that?

Those *eyes.* I think those eyes will be burned into my mind forever. They looked so familiar, so real, so infatuated. I've never been looked at like that before.

As the hot water soothes my skin, I think back to my past relationships, and the fact that I am not aware if they loved me. I thought they did, but maybe I was wrong. Even if they looked at me differently, was it the same way that I looked at them? I remember looking at them as if they were my world. Maybe they did love me, but it wasn't unconditionally. Maybe asking for unconditional feelings is too much. Maybe unconditional doesn't even exist.

Or maybe it does, just not for me.

"I don't think they're coming home today."

Or any day soon, for that matter.

Lara holds an ice pack to her head, "I'm starting to think your parents don't exist."

I sigh.

"I think something's happening. They've been gone for days."

My parents have always worked hard, harder than I assume they have to. I have never minded.

"Not necessarily a bad thing, you have more freedom," Lara replies.

I shrug.

"You didn't miss much last night. We went back to Grey's house," she chuckles and motions to her head. "Got a tiny bit buzzed, and then Cora and Grey completely disappeared."

"Disappeared?"

Lara grins slightly.

"Ah. So, we'll get the details whether we want them or not."

"Every single one," she sniffs and hands me the ice pack, jumping off of her seated place on the counter.

Even the smallest amount of weight in my hand causes my face to wince.

"You alright?"

I nod, "My arm is just a bit sore."

More than sore.

"Heroin?"

"Obviously."

Even if heroin still existed, I would be the last person expected to use it. Petrichor drugs are new, better. Healthy. The same effect, but less of the consequences. Still illegal for our age . . . but Grey and Lara tend not to adhere to that. We learned about them in school, the new ones and the old ones. It was an unusual lesson. Most of them are. During this specific lesson, though, I remember a student having to be led out. Her eyes became clouded with what she called memories, scratching her neck until it bled. She was soon admitted into the hospital and put on medication. Despite that accident, we still each had to do a project on the negative effects of the old drugs. Lara researched Heroin, and she tends to bring up her knowledge whenever she can.

If I mentioned anything else that indicated the rest of how I was feeling, maybe she would have thought I was actually on drugs.

No matter how much I try, I fail to remember anything after I left Paul's last night. I was walking, in my bed, and then dreaming. Hopefully, I just zoned out. I was tired, after all. Cause and effect.

But I remember the headache.

I remember the pain.

"Do you think they're in love?" I ask Lara abruptly, thinking back to my dream.

Lara glances at me for a moment, "Hell if I know."

"I think they are. At least Grey is."

She seems bored instantly. Lara isn't the love type.

And, as usual, she always has a way to change the subject.

"I have a surprise for you."

I glance at my arm, wishing only to go to sleep until the pain ebbs away.

"Should I be scared?"

I likely should be.

"Terrified."

Lara leads me up to my room. Natural light filters through the blinds and almost completely changes the space. Small bits of dust swirl throughout the sun's rays. They seem happy. The dust, I mean. Like they're in their element.

Lara clicks her tongue twice to get my attention. I stare, trying to comprehend the image in front of me.

She's holding a long, black dress. The look on her face makes it seem like it's for me. *Please* don't let it be for me.

"You're wearing it." She states.

I blink.

"What for?"

It's the only response I can think of.

"Try it on first," she whispers, holding the dress up to my chest.

⚜

Why have I never done this? I think to myself, examining the figure in the mirror. I can feel the confidence slowly rising in my chest. I welcome it. The dress fits me perfectly, and I don't know how Lara did it. I was hesitant at first, but now that has been completely replaced.

The dress is made out of thin satin. Not too tight, but not too loose. A slit runs up my leg to my mid-thigh, silver chains connecting the seams. It is sleeveless, though, which could potentially lead to something horrible.

"Well, now you have to come."

My eyebrow quirks.

She runs her fingers down the back of my arms, "You look like a new person."

Turning around, I observe the open back, similar chains running across my shoulder blades.

"It's a party," she quickly covers my mouth before I can speak, "and you're going."

A party. I do not like parties. Normally.

I sigh and look back at the mirror, "Okay."

I guess sleeping isn't the only way to ignore the lingering pain in my arm and in my head, right? The lingering dread of forgetting something you know you should be able to remember?

Her eyes grow wide, "Holy shit, did you say yes?"

I shrug, a small smile growing on my lips. I did.

"Hundred percent?"

I nod.

I mean, I do like how I look at the moment.

"It's with the group, Ignite."

"What? Wait but—"

"Shhhh, you already agreed. It's technically not even a group event. It's just a formal event at Paul's . . . and Ignite is attending. I thought you should go. Grey would be really happy. I would too, obviously. And I want to introduce you to someone, well not just someone . . . the one who runs it."

"The leader! Lara, they're not going to trust me—"

She interrupts once more, "It doesn't matter. I don't know why I was so worried about it, they'll love you," Lara looks at me up and down, "Cora will be there too, so you have three people to put in a good word."

She has a point.

I slowly nod. This is, in a way, what I wanted. Not to feel left out. I don't know what changed Lara's mind, whether it was Grey or something else, but I'm grateful.

"And, before you change your mind again, I'm doing your makeup . . . and hair."

"Wait, it's tonight? You failed to say that."

"Why else would I have wanted you to try it on now? No way in hell I would have told you about it too far in advance, you would have refused."

My confidence dwindles slightly, I didn't know I was that predictable.

"When does it start?"

She pulls some of my hair back, "Approximately twenty-five minutes ago."

Ah.

Great.

"Oh-my-fucking-god."

I purse my lips, trying to hide a smile that holds a tinge of narcissism.

I look good, I do. Lara was able to cover up most of the deadness in my appearance with her makeup talents. I look healthy.

Grey cups my face in his hands, "You look unreal."

His eyes scan mine affectionately. Silver and black eyeshadow covers the purple, tired look of my skin.

I look more mature; the hair helps with that. It's only straightened, but the thin metal twine that spirals around certain strands makes it look like I get ready for formal events every week. That I'm as confident as I wish people would see me as. The exact opposite of the way I actually am. The silver loops match my eyeshadow, jewelry, and the chains on my dress; Lara put a lot of thought into this.

Grey interlocks my arm in his, Lara already disappearing into the building.

"I'm glad she brought you. You finally get to meet him! Are you nervous?"

I shoot him a look, one of both confusion and annoyance. The confusion stems from the sudden mentioning of Ignite's leader by both Lara and Grey. Neither of them has spoken about him before tonight, and that coincidence has me worried.

He nods, "You, my friend, have nothing to worry about. You'll love him."

That's not why I'm nervous.

My stomach begins to drop as Grey takes a step towards the front gate. Something deep in my mind yells at me to keep going, but my body almost refuses to walk. I'm like a faulty magnet that doesn't know what it wants, partly being pulled towards the crowd and partly being pulled straight back to my house, the forest. The shed, for some unknown reason that I can't even begin to contemplate at the moment. Anywhere but here.

Chapter Nine

☙❦❧

March 27, 2073

9:30 PM

The crowd prevails.

Paul's is almost completely transformed. The artificial stars are dimmer now, gold. The dance floor remains, all except the fact that it's being used more as a place to converse than to dance. Gold streamers lace their way through the lights above us. Soft music plays as background noise.

I've learned about Greek gods before. Their personalities, their families, so on. I always liked to imagine what they looked like, ethereal beings. It's hard to find but a few possible depictions of them anymore; however, the scene in front of me provides quite a good substitute. It's insane, really. There are probably around fifty people, all dressed like they've been planning this for months. Some of the members even make me feel underdressed. Everyone's makeup shines in the light, almost like magic, complimenting their archaic smiles.

Grey sighs, "I should have done more, uh, *everything.*"

I look up at him, almost forgetting his height, especially with the platform boots he has on. He's unnaturally tall tonight. I scan his makeup: ice blue eyeshadow and body glitter underneath his jawline. He's wearing a sheer white button down, tucked into a long, light blue skirt. I guess he matched his colors just like Lara did for me.

If I were to make a list, he would be Zeus. Without the beard, obviously. Zeus had a beard, right? Grey wouldn't grow a beard even if the world was ending. Lara's words, not mine. Continuing the trend, I would say that she would be Athena, goddess of war. After all, her outfit is made purely of gold. The color, obviously, not the element.

As Lara and I were walking here, I attempted to get any information I could out of her about Ignite. I could tell she was hesitant, likely thinking that the more information I knew, the more likely it would be for me to turn around and stalk back home. However, based on her limited words about the subject, I didn't exactly have anything to fear. The group and its members were rather tame, not wishing to start fights with the government or even to draw unwanted attention to themselves at all. It's more a place where people can express their concerns or conspiracies and be met with similar opinions, which I guess could be consoling in a way. In essence, they don't outwardly *hate* Petrichor, and therefore wouldn't outwardly hate me because of my affiliations.

⁂

I have been stuck.

For thirty minutes.

"You believe that the people of this country are the only ones left?" I ask.

"Yes ma'am, that's why Petrichor watches us so closely. Don't want to turn out like the rest of the world, no ma'am."

"So you're in Petrichor's favor?" I ask.

"Absolutely not. Petrichor is the reason we're the only ones left. They killed the rest of the world."

Interesting. Though I guess there's no way to prove her wrong from my own experience, I've heard multiple friends of my parents speak about their vacations overseas.

"Oh," I nod sweetly. The fake smile burns my face. Grey had introduced me to an older lady with short white hair, one eye seemingly blind. She's been talking to me for about ten minutes, wringing her hands the whole time. She's extremely kind, definitely a talker though. I feel bad leaving. I really do. If I leave out of my own volition, she might believe it is her fault. It's not, I'm just nervous. About many things.

"Ira, darling, I have another person for you to meet," Grey snakes his arm around my hip at just the right time.

"It was nice to meet you," I shake the woman's hand as Grey pulls me away.

"What was her name again?" I whisper close to his ear.

"You think I know? I was hoping you would find out."

A horrible song begins to play as we walk. There's no rhythm, no vocals, just noise.

I shrug, he's been dragging me around the room since I first got here. I don't know how he already knows this many people but obviously he gets around.

"One more, I promise," Grey tilts my shoulders so that I'm facing him. "Hear me out on this one."

That doesn't sound good. Typically, this would mean he found a new prospect for himself, but because of Cora, this can only lead to one thing.

He has found a prospect for me.

Grey leads me toward the back of the room which has significantly fewer people and voices. Perhaps this is a good sign. As far as I can tell, there's only one person. He looks my age, at least close to it.

My suspicion returns intact.

"Ira, this is Tyl. Tyl, this is Ira."

I smile. My heart has not stopped pounding during this whole event, and I do not believe it will stop now. Not when I've found Apollo.

Curly blonde hair falling freely around his rounded face, some strands even gelled to look like ivy vines along his forehead and cheekbones. Dark skin causes his almost-golden eyes to truly glow. Even though he's shorter than Grey, I guess everyone is, he's still tall. Handsome.

He smiles gently, shaking my hand like it's porcelain, "I don't believe I've seen you at a previous meeting?"

A question, not a statement.

"Lara and I invited her," Grey answers for me.

Tyl nods, "It's very nice to meet you."

Genuine. The way his mouth slightly curved upward, never losing eye contact.

"Well," Grey claps his hands. "I'll leave you two to it."

"Oh, I-"

And he's gone.

He disappears into the crowd after giving me a discrete wink. At least, I hope it was discrete.

Tyl watches him go.

Of course, Grey left.

After standing a few moments of awkward silence, Tyl speaks up, "I assume he sprang this on you?"

I exhale, "It's been fun, though. Everyone is very welcoming."

Breathe.

"I meant talking to me," he chuckles, "but I'm glad you like the party."

Breathe.

"Oh," I inhale sharply. "He's been introducing me to a lot of people. It's okay though, everyone's been really nice."

I already said that. I already said that. I already said that.

"Did you talk to Grace?"

That was her name. Why couldn't I remember it?

"I did."

Breathe.

"I apologize," he whispers, silently laughing.

I smile, meeting his gaze. Tyl's eyes would almost be scary without the kind intention behind them. Either he's wearing colored contacts, or he really is Apollo. Or just blessed with amazing genes.

"Are you looking to join Ignite?"

"I . . . um. I'm not sure yet."

I should have said yes. He probably thinks I hate it here, that I hate him.

This is why I hate parties. The constant over analyzing, the questioning, the regret that comes when you get home and think of every single word you said or movement you made.

"No pressure. It's a good organization, I can promise that."

Lara waves at me from across the room, drink in hand. This is the first time I've seen her since we got here.

I wave back before returning my attention to Tyl. "How long have you been a part of it?"

Tyl swallows, standing up a bit straighter, "Since the beginning."

"That's impressive, you're dedicated." I can hear the shake in my voice as I try to keep a certain level of calm. I pray he cannot see through my wavering facade.

"It's very important to me."

I wait for him to explain why, but the silence remains.

Rubbing my arm, I watch Lara as she sifts through the crowd.

"I understand that this could be nerve wracking. It likely would be for me as well, if I was in your position. There's no judgment."

I snap my attention back to him, half expecting there to be a sarcastic grin. But of course, there's not, every word that comes out of his mouth is kind.

"Thank you. Everyone here is so connected; I don't want to impede."

He looks at me before shaking his head, "This group thrives on new members. But, again, no pressure."

I grin a bit, hard to help it when his smile is literally the sun.

"You must be close to the leader, being in it for so long and all."

There has to be a reason my friends mentioned the leader tonight.

Tyl smiles.

"I am the leader."

I blink, frozen upon his words.

I'm going to kill Grey.

When he notices the look on my face, he continues, "Technically my father started it, but when he passed, I decided to take it over." His voice hitches, causing me to break out of my murderous spell.

I give Tyl a tight smile, "Well, you've done a good job, for all these people to follow your cause."

He has. I can't imagine continuing a group like this, hosting events like this, while still attending class. Class is already stressful enough.

Tyl brightens, "Can I show you something? It's random, but you seem like you would find it interesting."

I mean, if it gets me out of here, away from the fake music and crowds, how could I say no? I like meeting new people, sure, but not when I'm forced.

"Sure." And something like relief steadies my breathing.

He tilts his head towards the archway before briskly leading me away, nodding politely at people as we go. I catch Grey's eye, a smirk appearing on his lips. I shake my head quickly. Whatever Grey wants to happen, it's not.

Before I know it, we're in the outdoor seating area. I've never seen it so deserted; it's usually packed every day of the year.

I follow him to the farthest table, watching his hair bounce as he walks, emphasized by his strides. I think he's doing it on purpose.

Tyl sits down in one of the chairs, motioning towards the one opposite him. When I sit, I realize my feet have been aching the whole night.

I needed this.

Whatever this is.

He sighs and looks up at the sky.

I do the same, waiting for him to speak. I do not want to be the first. I do not know what to say.

"I didn't really have anything to show you. I figured you wanted to get out of there."

Something starts to awake in my chest.

Appreciation, I believe.

"Thank you, was it that obvious?" I look down at my hands, fighting a smile.

"A bit, but it's the least I can do. I get overwhelmed at events sometimes too, and I'm the one hosting them."

A corny statement, but I fake a laugh nonetheless.

Tyl runs a delicate hand through his hair, rubbing the back of his neck, "Are Grey and Cora together?"

Random.

I nod, "Very recently."

"I like them together. They make a good match."

It's hard to miss the hint of sadness to his voice.

"Do you know Cora well?" I ask.

"They've been a part of this group for a while." Tyl sits up straighter. "But besides that, I don't really know a lot of their history. They keep it professional, granted, but they are close with my family."

"I could see Cora as a family person," I respond, but quickly wish that I could take it back. I don't know why I said that. I barely know anything about them, definitely not enough to know whether or not they put their family first.

But, Tyl doesn't seem to mind, "my younger sister loves them."

I smile briefly, not exactly sure how to respond. He remains staring into the sky.

"I don't have any siblings."

I close my eyes. Why did I say that? Unnecessary.

"A blessing and a curse."

Sure, I guess. Though I don't envy the lesser amount of alone time that it seems people with siblings endure.

"You know, not all of the meetings are like this. If you are thinking about joining, I don't want you to think that every week you'll have to dress up and mingle with people you don't know," he looks at me, "I know that many wouldn't like that."

"Then what are the usual meetings like?" I ask, returning his gaze.

"Still a lot of talking, but with casual clothes and in a much smaller space. But, if you would rather just listen, no one forces you to speak. Its discussion based."

"What kind of discussions?"

His eyes turn thoughtful, "well, as of right now, we've been talking about something that's been happening recently, to a lot of people. It's been kept on the down low, I'm not exactly sure how or why, but it scares the majority of us, me most of all."

Well damn.

I stare at him, trying to decide whether or not he's waiting on me to ask what it is, or if he doesn't exactly trust me enough to share the details.

"I'm sorry," Tyl shakes his head, smiling a bit, "That got dark, and unintentionally mysterious. I just didn't want to go off on a tangent if it would be boring for you."

I can already feel my heart melting.

"No, please, now I'm curious."

He lowers his voice a bit, "only if you say so."

I nod, gesturing for him to continue.

"There's always been memory issues when it comes to the older community, the air pollution explanation, all of that. But recently we keep hearing experiences of it beginning to happen to people who were born way after Petrichor rose to power. Grace, the woman you were speaking to, her granddaughter has started to mix up experiences, some real and some not, and no one knows where it came from or how it started. When Grace took her to the doctor, they said very little besides prescribing rest. They said her granddaughter was just stressed, and maybe that's true, but there's something else going on. There are multiple family members of Ignite that are having similar issues."

I don't know what I was expecting, but it definitely wasn't that. How have I not heard about this? How is this not a well-known issue at this point, especially if it's happening to so many people in such a small area? Is it another issue with air pollution? Petrichor swears all of that has been fixed, but then what could cause this? Why . . . why don't more people know about this?

Before I can respond to Tyl, I hear something crash behind me, sending my nerves into a frenzy. A flash of pain shoots throughout my neck as I try to turn around as quickly as possible. Too fast, apparently. Grey is laying on the ground, laughing, right next to a tipped-over chair. Lara leans on the table above him, attempting yet failing to look nonchalant.

Typical.

And just like that, I decide to postpone my worries for a later time. A time where perhaps I can actually talk to Tyl alone about it. About the severity.

But, for right now, there's no use.

"They were spying on us?"

I squeeze my lips shut, trying not to laugh, "I believe they were."

"Do you two mind giving us a couple of minutes?" Tyl asks, loudly enough for them to hear over the distance and the music.

I stare at him, and he winks at me. Lara takes off into the building as Grey jumps up, giving us a small bow before following.

I turn back, slowly this time, to face him.

"If they're expecting something, I give you full permission to make up a story," he snorts, leaning back in his chair.

"I don't think they would believe me even if I did."

"Ah," he quirks an eyebrow, "what if we stargazed and danced until our feet hurt and then we finally had one extremely romantic kiss under the moonlight?" Tyl frowns when I don't respond, "Too much, maybe?"

I chuckle, "Sounds a bit like an old movie. They would expect me to make something up like that."

"Seems like I've found someone interested in the past as well." He smiles.

As well. He's interested as well?

I look down at my hands, "I'm glad I found someone that enjoys it too."

Is this flirting?

"Did you think I made up that whole date off the top of my head? Maybe I should have said I did, more impressive that way."

"Impressive either way," I grin.

I have never really found anyone that was interested in the old world, a good portion are even scared of it, don't even like to talk about it. As if it's taboo.

"I used to—"

A crack of a twig sounding from the woods steals my attention away. I don't think animals would come this close to Paul's, and even if they did, it wouldn't be one large enough to produce that sound.

I pause, scanning the trees in front of us. I definitely would not appreciate dying tonight. Even though there's hardly any crime around this area, especially this area, paranoia creeps through me like a disease. It always has, in suspenseful moments like this.

"For someone who's apparently interested in a multitude of romantic topics, the music that you play at your parties is absolute shit."

My headache returns with a ferocious roar, likely stemming from the fact that my heart could beat out of my chest at any moment.

"Sorry?" Tyl stands.

The mysterious voice remains hidden in the shadow of a tree. "My apologies, I suppose that came off very harsh. Let me try again. If you want to take a girl back home with you, start by playing music that's actually enjoyable. And then, perhaps, work on your comedy skills. There's much left to be desired."

Red flushes my cheeks as I keep my gaze locked on the darkness. Even without the face to match the voice, the sarcasm still rings clear.

Tyl's jaw clenches, "Luckily, I'm not the one who chose the music. If you have a complaint, you can talk to Paul's. Or, if you have a complaint that has to do with me, maybe we could talk personally? Alone?"

I really don't know how he does it. Tyl could say anything and it would come across like smooth gold. Even though he's struggling to remain calm and polite, his voice doesn't show any hints of conflict.

The unknown being begins to fully appear now, slowly making its way towards the light of the lanterns.

Hades.

I believe I found Hades.

Or, actually, rediscovered.

Hades is the boy from Fern's, the thief, the one that took the records, Izmene's contact. Mystery man.

And he's here.

Now.

He is around our age as well, perhaps closer to Tyl's than mine. Dark brown waves of hair cascade around his face, stopping abruptly above his shoulders in layers. It seems like he put a lot of work into his appearance, specifically his hair, even though the bottom edges are beginning to curl. I wonder if his hair is as curly as Tyl's. If it is, they would almost be ironic. So similar yet so different. The black suit helps, completely contrasting the light blue one standing next to me. Hades almost looks as if he's a shadow hoping to disguise as a human; someone that stands out against the rest of the members inside.

The smiles are different too.

Tyl's is welcoming, friendly, and powerful all at once. Well, I guess the black suit's smile is powerful too, but in a different way. He shows no teeth, no welcoming brilliance; a full, cryptic grin.

It's intriguing, but not in the best meaning of the term.

Maybe the worst meaning.

He continues to walk towards us as we stay completely silent, staring at Tyl as if he's the odd one out. Hades doesn't even spare me a glance.

"Who do you know here?" Tyl asks.

The boy gives Tyl a look of sarcastic offense before sitting down beside me without invitation. I refuse to make eye contact, though I doubt he would try, and pointedly stares at his polished black shoes instead. A safety pin hangs off one of the laces. That one singular safety pin is the only sign of a personality that I can observe; it matches his earrings.

"No one. I came with the intent of joining Ignite, but I suppose if it's run by a child, I might need to reconsider."

If Tyl didn't seem as confused as me, I would have thought they already knew each other. Some lifelong grudge.

"You seem the same age."

I can see Hades's head quickly turn my way out of my peripheral vision. I assume he's surprised that I spoke to him; honestly, I am too. The same feelings return from when I saw him before, constricting my chest and filling it with something close to anger. Close to grief, a feeling I cannot explain the origin of even if I wanted to.

Hades taps his foot against the rocks, speaking to me, "I didn't come here to chat or talk about ages; age does not mean maturity or experience. But I suppose when it comes to the latter, I can assume you're extremely lacking."

I hold my breath.

"Have I given you a reason not to trust me, or has anyone else?" Hades asks as Tyl forces the boy's attention back to himself.

Hades begins to twirl a strand of hair.

"That's a different question. I'm not judging based on trust, I'm judging based on facts . . . I suppose words as well."

Tyl laughs gently, "If you don't agree with me leading this organization, then why are you still here?"

My jaw clenches. I force myself to look up, waiting for Hade's response. Tyl's eyes are set, a mix of amusement and restraint. The other holds a similar stare, just without the restriction.

"I want to be proved wrong," Hades makes eye contact with me, "and besides, why not help a failing organization? I would hate to see Ignite fall before I'm able to provide information for once in its upsetting history."

I close my eyes involuntarily in hopes that the stillness will ease the anger. I've never felt this before. Does he do this to everyone? Bring out the worst emotion?

It's terrifying.

There are many reasons for the way I feel, one of them being the unnecessary hostility towards Tyl, who I don't personally think could ever hurt a soul. To be honest, I don't even care about the comment towards me. His eyes, much like Cora's and Izmene's, radiate with an unmatched energy; and, in this instance, they seem primed to kill. Matching his gaze makes my anger, my discomfort even more unbearable. His gaze does not fill me with curiosity, it fills me with some form of resentment. I have heard of this happening to other people, especially Lara. She speaks often about meeting someone once and already disliking them, making a quick judgment of character. I have always thought she was being too hasty, but maybe I was wrong. "What's your name?"

Tyl looks at me, searching my face for something unknown. Maybe he's trying to figure out why I just asked that question.

"Like I said, I'm not here to chat."

"Answer her," Tyl states in an impressively deep tone. "It's a simple question."

After a long pause between tension, Hades finally states his name. His name is E.

Short for something, obviously, but I honestly couldn't care less. All I needed was something to call him.

Tyl finally sits back down, "This is Meira, and I'm—"

"If I didn't already know your name, I would have asked for it," E interjects.

I purse my lips, praying for this to stop soon. I hate confrontation.

Extreme silence attempts to answer my wish, only making this worse in the process. I look back down. Why couldn't Grey and Lara have interrupted now instead of mere minutes ago?

But, to my surprise, and to my relief, they actually do.

Maybe I'm psychic. That would be useful.

"Who's this?" Grey mouths, tilting his head towards E.

I shrug and raise my eyebrows, trying to send some type of warning. I'm as bad at giving signals as I am receiving them.

Grey takes his place behind me, both hands on the back of my chair. "I've never seen you before."

He doesn't remember him from Fern's, apparently. Likely a good thing, I would not want this interaction to be more awkward than it already is.

"Odd, because I've seen you," E tilts his head towards Lara, who's sitting in the last remaining chair at the table. "And you."

"We've met before?"

Based on the twisted grin, I can assume that this was just the type of question he was waiting on.

"As I told your leader here, I have information that can help this group."

Tyl exhales. A delicate muscle twitches close to his lip.

"You know him?" Lara asks, gesturing to the Death god looming around us all.

"No," Tyl chooses his words carefully, "but he nonetheless seems to have multiple complaints about the management of Ignite, specifically about me."

That's all Lara needs to hear. Quick judgment of character, as I've stated.

"Is that so? Based on my professional opinion, I say that you're an asshole and Ignite can find information on its own."

I think my teeth might shatter if I bite down any harder. I should have known that Lara would make the tension even higher. She never backs down, especially with people like E. His grin becomes wider now, and he is slowly reaching for his blazer pocket.

E slams a dark brown bottle onto the table, something called Root Beer.

"You shouldn't be drinking that here," Tyl whispers, and I can see Lara lean towards the bottle out of the corner of my eye.

E looks at all of us slowly, analyzing, before slightly rolling his eyes, "It's soda. I could stain that dashing suit of yours if you wish to double check."

I squint to read the label. Non-alcoholic.

Root beer is a stupid name for it then.

I've never heard of it before. I don't think any of us have.

"Do you ever speak, besides the occasional unhelpful questions?"

It took me a moment to realize the jab was aimed towards me.

"What?" I ask, caught completely off guard.

E slides his chair closer to mine, "I asked you a question. You've added barely nothing to this thrilling conversation."

I can't read the emotions in his eyes.

"Her silence adds more to this conversation than any of your words," Grey finally speaks up.

A small smile breaks on my lips. He seems to notice, leaning his elbows on his knees. I attempt to keep his gaze.

"Do you think I should join, angel, or do you agree with them?" E whispers gently, staring into my soul. There's something in his eyes that matches the soft change of his voice. Like the beach when it changes from day to night, seeming almost like a completely different place.

I've always liked the beach better at night.

Also, *what* did he call me?

"I can't really say, I'm not a part of it."

"Answer the question."

I glance around, silently pleading for help. Please let this one signal get across.

"She shouldn't have to answer that. It's not her decision, and it won't be yours soon either unless you explain why you're here, besides to complain."

Thank God for Tyl.

"You two should just hook up already and get it over with," E leans his head back, looking up to the stars, "if I need to prove myself to you, I know how Petrichor truly got started. Believe me or not, that's up to you. From what I've heard, everything they're telling you is bullshit, and this group seems like it really wants to get off the ground, to actually do something as opposed to just sit around and join hands, but you need answers to do that. If you want the truth, I have it. All I ask in return is that you help me find out who's leading it, even though after meeting all of you I'm sure useful assistance is a lost cause."

I choose to ignore the first part. If he isn't lying about the rest, this could change everything. Part of me is curious; I mean, I always have been. The other part of me is scared; do we really need to know the answer? "How can you possibly know how Petrichor got started if you don't know who runs it?" Lara asks, shooting me a quick, apologetic glance. I think it became a habit not to talk about Petrichor in front of me. "Some answers are easier to find than others," E replies.

I watch as questions start to hurl towards him, one after another. "How do we know you aren't lying?" "Where did you get that information?" "You were the one that stole food from Fern's, weren't you?" That was from Grey. Questions begin to flow. "Why do you want to know who leads it?" "Was stealing the food really necessary?" and so forth.

E takes a long sigh, "If we have an agreement, I can answer all of those, except the ones about Fern's. You decide."

Tyl inhales, "We try to keep this group as calm as possible. We don't want trouble with the government, most of us just want answers. Do you understand?" His voice is stern, clouded with emotion, yet still somehow polite.

"That's a tough requirement. I was like you once, hated violence, but progress will not be made without risks. The root of human nature is violence, same with Petrichor." E responds.

Tyl ignores him.

I don't know what the 'root of human nature is,' but I know it's not violence. I assume it's a weak excuse for him to remain angry at all times. Angry at humanity.

"Do you *understand?*"

"Absolutely."

The glint in E's eyes shows quite the opposite. I remain silent, maybe I'm wrong. It's not my choice to make anyways. This is up to Tyl.

He seems to have noticed the mysterious gleam in E's eyes as well, "You can come to the next meeting, only if you continue to remember what I said," Tyl says.

I bite the inside of my cheek, feeling guilty for wishing to join them as well.

Lara tilts her head, watching something far behind me. I turn around as Grey rushes to the archway to meet Cora, who welcomes him with a smile. He wraps his arm around them, whispering something in their ear. Cora nods and motions back to the party, disappearing quickly.

"I should go," E sighs.

The sudden voice almost scares me, I almost forgot E was there. When I look back at E, however, my emotions change. The blood is completely drained from his face, leaving him insanely pale, staring at the archway.

He tucks his hair quickly behind his ears, moving to stand.

"Why so sudden?" Lara asks sarcastically, leaning back in her chair, "We'll miss you."

E ignores her and whispers close to my ear, "Your quietness doesn't hide anything, don't act as if it does. You're terrible at hiding what you feel."

He runs two calloused fingers down his bicep before turning to leave and disappearing back to the street. I glance down at my own arm, noticing for the first time the crescent moon indentations left by my nails.

Blinking, the world slows around me. I almost feel like I can read E better than I've ever been able to read someone before, but I didn't expect him to be able to do the same.

Chapter Ten

March 30, 2073

12:00 PM

"And then he left?" I grind my palms against my eyelids, "Yes, after he saw Cora and Grey."

"I didn't realize Cora was there," Izmene sets down a transparent blue record, the tension in her shoulders suddenly apparent. She won't look at me.

"Sorry, I forgot to mention that. They were busy so I didn't get to talk to them much."

After explaining what happened that night to Izmene for about forty-five minutes, I was bound to forget something. It had been almost three days, but I felt like I needed to speak about it to someone who wasn't there. An outside perspective. Typically, I'm able to bottle everything in, to process everything myself, but not that night. Definitely not that night. To begin, half of my mind can't stop thinking about Tyl. How is he able to accomplish so much when I feel like I barely have time to do anything, especially when school is in session? How was he so nice, so easily? He could tell I wanted to leave, and even though it was his own party, he led me outside so I would be able to escape it. Tyl knew because he feels the same things, he has the same reactions to people and interactions that I do and I've never had that with anybody else. It was relaxing, it was refreshing, but also unnerving. Was I supposed to know what his end goal was? Was Tyl just being nice? Was E right in his constant jabs?

E.

Him.

He was the subject of the other half of my mind. It's like I can't escape him. He's everywhere. I wouldn't be surprised if I go home today and he's sitting at my desk. Not only that, but how could he make all of those comments to people he doesn't know? All of the assumptions about Tyl's leadership and my . . . what did he even say? Experience? E doesn't know Tyl. He doesn't know me, but at the same time, he does. He noticed my nails digging into my arm. He noticed even when I didn't.

How am I supposed to explain that? To understand that?

I've been working as much as I can, even when Izmene doesn't ask me to come in. She's here seemingly every day, so I never have to worry about the door being locked or other people assuming I'm wandering around. She never minds when I come in unannounced, or at least, she doesn't show it. She's confused each time, but that's about it. Izmene has almost become a lifeline, someone who I can talk to and never feel as if it will have implications further down the road. Not that I don't feel that when talking to Lara and Grey, but, it's easy to talk to Izmene. It's different.

"Cora is always busy," she tries to laugh, but it comes across painfully forced, "I haven't been able to talk to them in a while myself."

"Isn't Cora here a lot?"

That's what Grey said.

"Only for an hour or two. They are a floater. They go where help is needed."

Vague.

I'll have to ask Grey if helping people around the area is actually Cora's job somehow, or if they're just a generous person.

Maybe both.

I smooth the last sticker across an album cover, skimming the address as I do. We recently switched from handwriting the labels to using a label-maker, which I am quite happy about. I never would have mentioned it, but by the end of the day my hand was always sore from writing. Luckily, the arm pain is almost all but faded. The headache still remains, but that is much easier to ignore.

Izmene still insists on keeping most of this operation under wraps, but I've gathered a little information here and there. I know that there are two people, their code names being Bird and Cliff, that deliver the records to houses. I started to notice that one of those two names was always written above the address, along with a sticky note on one of the crates that read "Bird's substitute delivery." I connected the dots myself. Maybe I'm completely wrong, but I like to think I'm Sherlock Holmes. That's his name, right? The detective? Sounds right. At first, I thought that maybe one of them might be E, but Izmene said the records that he took were his, not that he was delivering them. And unless she's lying, which might be a possibility, I assume he's not a part of this. I hope he's not a part of this. But, at the same time, why wouldn't she explain why we're delivering them to people my age as well? She completely avoided the question. But, Izmene's been so generous, I feel bad asking again.

Also, I failed to learn in all of my time in the library that Cora doesn't work here full time or even what would qualify as part time.

Maybe they're Cliff or Bird?

They seem like a Bird to me.

If that were true, I don't know why Izmene wouldn't just tell me.

I don't know why she doesn't just tell me a lot of things.

". . . I try to keep up with Cora but they move at a hundred beats per minute."

I swallow, realizing that Izmene was still speaking.

"I didn't know that you were close with them."

It seems like Cora is close to everybody. Grey, Tyl's family, now Izmene? I knew they worked in the same place, but nothing more.

Izmene bites her lip, eyes darkening in thought, "I didn't tell you?"

I wrack my mind for anything that Izmene has mentioned about Cora, but nothing comes to mind. Maybe my memory isn't reliable anymore.

"Cora is my grandchild."

I pause.

She very much did not tell me that.

I feel my stomach drop. God, does it run in the family or something? I should have realized it sooner. I definitely should have realized it sooner. I mean, even their hair is similar.

"That makes a lot of sense, actually."

That was all I could come up with.

Izmene smiles shortly before turning to walk away.

At this point, what's stopping me? I know Izmene well enough to guess she won't be upset at personal questions. Maybe at questions she's already tried to avoid, but not personal questions. Hopefully. Besides, it involves me too. Or, at least, it might involve me.

"Have we met before? You, Cora, and I? Maybe when I was younger?" I ask.

It would explain the feelings I get from them, the easiness it is to talk to them.

Izmene pauses, adjusting the hem of her dress.

As she moves to look me in the eye, all I can see is pain. Not normal pain. Unfiltered pain. Raw pain. Pain that's scratching to escape but is held in place by some sort of invisible barrier.

"If we have, I would have remembered you."

Before I have time to react, the door is already shut. My chest rises and falls.

It was not normal pain that I saw reflected, but true pain. Pain that I caused.

I shouldn't have asked.

I know I shouldn't have asked.

"How did you not know that?"

"I mean, I didn't either."

"That's because you're an unobservant little shit."

Lara throws an ice pack at Grey's head, "Say it again."

He barely has time to duck, but he succeeds, smoothly flipping her off in the process. Apparently, something happened at the party that I wasn't aware of, even though they seemed completely fine when I was with them. Sometimes I think they just come up with things to be mad about. For example, a month ago, Grey ran into my house crying, sobbing into my pillow for an hour stating that he would never speak to Lara again. I laid there with him until he was ready to speak, but at that point he had already forgotten what had happened.

"Did Cora tell you or did you assume that they were Ismene's grandchild?" I ask quietly, hoping to ease the conversation back down.

Grey shrugs, "both. I could tell they looked alike before Cora told me. Explains why Izmene is a 'gilf'."

"That's extremely fucked up. Does Cora know about your inappropriate fantasies about their *grandmother?*"

A smug grin appears on his face, "They do, actually. They think it's funny."

I pinch the bridge of my nose, not in annoyance, but tiredness.

"If you really want to hear a fantasy, I could tell you what happened after the party with Cora and I, we—" Grey offers.

"Ah! Zip it. We agreed you wouldn't talk about shit like that unless we asked."

Grey stomps his foot on the ground, about to throw a fake tantrum, "You guys are no fun."

"Are we as fun as E?"

Grey loses his facade when he senses my sarcasm, "don't mention his name, or lack thereof. A letter is not a name. He might have been hot when I first saw him at Fern's, but not with a fucking personality like that."

Lara rolls her eyes, "He was thrilling. We could never reach that level even if we tried."

"So thrilling," Grey chimes in, "that we left five minutes after he did. Never thought anyone would take away the appeal of a party, but alas. Even Tyl looked like he wanted to drop dead."

Respectively. Tyl still looked as polite as ever afterwards, but even I could see the mask breaking. It was something about E's gaze, the way he looked like he wanted to simultaneously kill us and make us bow.

Grey isn't exaggerating about the timing though. After E disappeared, we sat in silence until Lara finally decided that it was time to leave. It was a good call. Tyl bade us good night, giving me a brief hug beforehand. Lara made a big deal out of it . . . she shouldn't have. It didn't feel like a romantic hug, which isn't a bad thing. It was comforting.

But, for both Lara and Grey, it was much more.

"How long do you give it?"

Grey rubs his chin in exaggeration, examining my face as if it's a painting in a museum.

"You know, Lara, I'm gonna say two weeks."

Lara sighs, leaning a careful arm over his shoulder, most likely trying to decide whether or not he's still mad. Apparently, her olive branch, which is talking about Tyl and I, works famously.

"I'll give it one."

He gasps, "You have no hope for the girl."

"Look into her eyes, Grey, there's something there."

If there is something there, it's remnants of confusion from earlier today, not last night, "I think you two are desperate."

"Ah, see right there," Lara tuts, "where did that attitude come from, huh?"

Grey takes my jaw in his hand, moving it around to examine my neck.

"No hickies."

I swat his arm away, "We just met."

"And?"

"It's always the polite ones," Lara shrugs, picking up a pen from my desk to write on her hand after failing in her search for paper.

"What's *always* the polite ones, Lara? Enlighten me. It might be good for Ms. Innocent over here to listen as well."

He knows I hate when people call me that. Just because I haven't experienced certain things doesn't mean I don't understand them. Besides Lara and Grey, people don't seem to understand that.

Lara starts to count off her fingers, "Tyl is the leader of Ignite."

"Which means he's controlling," Grey finishes.

They begin to go back and forth, finishing each other's sentences. It's happened before.

"He's smart."

"Which means he knows some tricks."

"He's demanding."

"That one's self-explanatory."

"I mean, you two could always date him," I interrupt, a grin plastering itself across my face despite the situation.

"Can't. Not my type."

"Can't. In a relationship," Grey raises his eyebrows, "which leaves . . ."

Lara flips her palm towards me to reveal words in smudgy black ink.

Pros: everything . . . you know, especially everything ;)
Cons: nothing

"You two could be completely wrong."

"About him being kinky? Doubt it."

"No, Grey," I take the pen from Lara and quickly write on my forearm.

We could just stay friends.

"I know damn well that's not how you work."

Perhaps.

"You're gonna fall in love with him." Lara grabs the pen and returns it to my desk.

I'm not.

But he is nice.

But he does like old movies.

But he is attractive.

But he isn't . . .

My mind blanks.

"All I ask is that you'll think about it, especially considering the fact that there might just be an Ignite meeting tomorrow that you're invited to."

What?

"What do you mean I'm invited?"

Lara and Grey exchange more glances, grinning from ear to ear until Grey finally explains, "Tyl came to me personally, he wants you to go tomorrow to feel things out."

Oh god.

Do I want to go? Yes. Do I feel as if I'll be betraying my parents? Also, yes.

But, at the same time, it doesn't seem as if Ignite wants to start problems. They just want answers, which I do too.

I want a lot of answers.

My parents likely wouldn't even know I went, it's not as if they can message me through their Tirn considering they left theirs here. I guess the issue lies more with Ignite finding out about my parents and where they work. I don't want them to feel as if they can't trust me, especially Tyl. But, at the same time, maybe me going to the meeting in the first place might show I can be trusted. Unless they think I'm spying . . . but why would I do that? Why would . . .

I need to calm down.

"What's the worst that can happen? The party wasn't a real meeting, so you're not allowed to make judgments. Try it out," there is a hint of pleading in his voice, or maybe hope. He always feels bad whenever anyone questions Petrichor in front of me, though I know he's not Petrichor's biggest fan. Perhaps me going to this meeting shows him that I'm fine with him talking about it, with anyone talking about it. At least I hope it will.

"I'll go, only if I don't have to talk."

Maybe this was actually a good decision. We've been here for about five minutes and I haven't come up with any excuses yet as to why I should leave.

The meetings, according to Lara and Grey, are always held at different parks, except if it's raining of course. If it's raining, it's held at Tyl's house.

Part of me wishes it was raining.

However, I do love this park.

There are many more people in this group than I thought. While the majority of them seem to be around our own age, there are some older adults as well. Surprisingly, even though there are a lot of people, I still don't necessarily want to leave.

Especially because all of these people are looking to one specific individual—Tyl.

Tyl.

He looks like he was made to be a leader.

I haven't gotten to speak to him yet, as he's been making his rounds with virtually everyone. They all seem to worship him, shaking his hand and laughing along with what he says. Tyl isn't dressed up in any way, just wearing a simple white T-shirt and khaki pants, but if an outsider were to look in, they would immediately know who the leader was. It's in his confidence, in his smile, in everything that he does.

"So, you did decide to show up? Speaking of which, I'm glad you're here."

"As am I. Lara and Grey convinced me, and I guess your invitation too."

He winks, "We're about to start actually, but feel free to stay over here if you like. I know it looks cult-ish, but there's really no other way to sit out here. I promise we're not a cult, at least that I know of."

When Tyl laughs, it sounds like the epitome of perfection. My mind almost didn't even contemplate the cult part at first, though now I'm a bit concerned.

Tyl says something to the crowd that I don't quite hear, as Grey grabs my hand, "let's go."

"But he said I could stay over here."

"You're here to feel it out, so come feel it out."

To my dismay, Lara doesn't come to my rescue. She only shrugs.

Perhaps this might be my first strike.

Three strikes and I leave. Deal? Deal.

Yes, I came to feel it out but I never planned on participating. Especially now that I understand what Tyl was talking about.

They sit in a circle.

One big circle. On the ground.

Cult-like indeed.

Luckily, though for an unknown reason, Grey leads me across the circle from Tyl. Even though I might enjoy sitting close to him, I don't want that many eyes on me.

"So you can see him in all of his glory," Grey whispers into my ear.

"You're insane," I snap back.

Lara says nothing.

I haven't exactly talked to her about it, but I don't think she's comfortable with me being here. She's so used to not even speaking about Petrichor in front of me. I mean, hell, she tried to hide one of the meetings from me last time and now she brought me straight into the lion's den. Maybe when Lara sees that I'm alright with being here, and that I'm actually enjoying myself, maybe she'll calm down. Unless, of course, there's three strikes.

And number two just sat down next to me.

"You're late."

So it begins.

E grins, turning his gaze on Lara, "it's hard to be late when there's nothing to miss. I assume, based on the lack of speaking, that I haven't missed anything?"

No one responds.

"Precisely," E's smile widens.

Tyl's voice sounds suddenly, catching everyone's attention, "I hope everyone is well, and that you had a good time at the party . . ." His eyes slide to me.

Which was a mistake.

"Well, did you have a good time at the party, angel?" E's voice is quiet as Tyl continues to speak to the rest of the group.

"Yes, for a bit."

I can sense his smile without even looking.

"Before I got there, you mean? Pity."

He's not wrong, not in the slightest.

All I can do is roll my eyes.

"Are you cold?"

"I'm trying to listen."

"You have cold chills on your arms."

"It's cold outside," I respond, my frustration peaked.

"So, you are cold?"

"Yes, because half of my wardrobe doesn't consist of black sweaters."

He is, indeed, wearing a black sweater.

"So you do pay attention?"

"To you? Hardly."

I know what he's doing. I know that he's only trying to rile me as he did with everyone else at the party, and I hate every part of it.

But mostly, I hate the fact that it works.

I hate the fact that every time I even look at him all I want to do is scream.

E frustrates me on a level I didn't know possible, and I've barely even spoken to him. It boils down to his arrogance and the hatred, behind every word. It's as if he's never met another person worthy of his liking, his grace.

"You let her speak like this?" E whispers towards Lara and Grey

"Like what?" Grey spits back.

"Cruel."

I can almost hear my heart hammering in my chest.

"Meira has never been cruel to anyone. If you're the first, you probably deserve it."

He locks his gaze with mine.

After all that he's said, he calls me the cruel one?

"I never said I didn't deserve it." E responds.

Lara just scoffs, so does Grey, but now I'm stuck here attempting to figure out why he's able to act how he acts, say what he says, and then call me *cruel*.

"E, welcome to Ignite. Everyone, this is E, last time we spoke he told me he had important information to share."

Tyl's voice is like a sharp wind, pulling our attention back to the other side of the circle.

I can sense E's body stiffen beside me,

"I don't remember stating I would share this publicly." E responds

"You said you had information for Ignite. This is Ignite. Share." Tyl retorts.

I blink.

"Demanding," Grey whispers, nudging me with his elbow.

I can't refrain from looking between E and Tyl, neither of them backing down, staring at each other through unflinching gazes.

Eventually, E sighs, "Fine."

Part of me thought the tension would never end. They're both like two sides of the same coin, confident and intimidating in different ways.

Perhaps they would have been friends in another life.

"Go ahead."

E laughs under his breath. He acts as if all eyes aren't on him, surveying him, testing him. Seeing if he'll tell the truth, if he's worth it.

"Are you willing to trust me?"

"Depends on what you say."

"And if I said I knew how Petrichor was founded, the truth behind it?"

Someone from the group, an older man with a hint of a goatee, chimes in, "we likely wouldn't believe you."

I don't know how he even expects us to believe him, to want to give him a chance.

E shrugs, "I'll explain what I know, it is your choice whether or not to believe me."

Silence.

Even the trees seem to be waiting for E to continue.

"The corruption of the Earth was real, but it was not as large of a group effort as your government played it out to be. Everyone had a part, yes, but the majority was caused by people who knew what would happen. They wanted it to happen, so that they could be the heroes. They would swoop in and fix everything, rebuild the goddamn world if they had to, only to garner power. Everything was for power. The founders wanted people to owe them, they wanted everyone to owe them, to lean on them for anything and everything, all so that no matter what they did, there would be no questions. It was all built on false pretense. By gaining the people's trust, they were able to take power because they were the only ones who knew how to fix what was happening. They used fear, it was all fear."

Inhale.

Exhale.

There are two options.

If E is telling the truth, if he somehow knows this for certain . . .

I don't know what to think. We would all have to come to terms with the fact that our whole world is built on lies, that the supposed heroes were anything but. They might have been the saviors, but they were also the cause.

If E is lying, it would make this whole situation a hell of a lot easier.

"How are we supposed to prove that's true?" Lara asks as many other members nod alongside her question.

"Why would I lie?" E responds.

I could think of a multitude of different reasons. For fun, to be annoying, to be *cruel* . . .

"You said at the party that you wanted our help in attempting to find the leader, you might just have bullshitted us simply so that we would lend it to you." Grey responds.

E doesn't even look at Grey, "Perhaps, but that's boring. If I was only stringing everyone along for help, I would have come up with something much more interesting."

Tyl shakes his head, "Then tell us how you know this."

Please tell us how you know this.

"Look around you. Look at everything that all of you have adjusted to. There are no elections, there are no choices, you all follow Petrichor blindly without question, while they continue to take things away until you forget that you ever had them in the first place. They have taken away everything that could be used against them. No phones anymore, barely any music, movies, anything. If you think it is for your own wellbeing, for the world's wellbeing, then so be it. I'm only asking you to observe. Observe everything."

The silence that follows isn't like the one previously, it's not waiting, but thinking. Everyone is thinking. About the old world, about the one we live in, or perhaps lack-thereof.

The old man continues, "I'm still confused as to why you told us this. If it's true, you've given us a lot of power, though to start a revolt—"

'Which we won't be doing," Tyl responds to the older man.

"I need to figure out the leader's identity, and I'm hoping that with information that every one of you gains from everyday life I'll be able to piece it together." E says.

"You think you can piece together something that no one else has in fifty years? What makes you so different?" I question.

My voice sounds quieter than the rest, but I can't help it. I'm too busy attempting to understand the implications of everything that E has said, everything that he wishes to accomplish.

"Care to find out?" E asks.

No. No I do not.

"Give us a reason to trust you, E. More than just observations about the world."

Tyl looks worried, likely because of his wish to avoid any trouble with the government. If, somehow and someway, E does figure out who the leader is and everyone here assisted him, I don't know what that would mean. Are we in the wrong? Is E? Or is our government?

We just want answers to our questions. That's all.

E looks around the group until his eyes land back on me, "I can't."

"Can't, or won't?" I respond.

"Both. But I swear if I find the leader, I will be able to prove it. I will be able to prove all of it."

Tyl nods, "for the sake of this meeting not lasting until midnight, let's say that we do end up helping you. What do we have to do?"

"Tell me about your days, about life with Petrichor. Tell me about conspiracies or theories, anything."

"Why are our lives any different than yours? You live in Petrichor's world as well."

E shakes his head, "not in the same way."

What is that supposed to mean?

If I were to take a guess, I would say he lives in a bunker, alone. Hating everyone. Everything. But, at the moment, I can't say I would blame him.

"Do you know about the memory loss?"

E stares down Grace, "the what?"

"The memory loss issues," she continues, "they used to only happen to people my age, but now it seems like it's spreading. My granddaughter . . ."

Her voice trails off as the people seated around her try to console.

"Your granddaughter is losing her memory?"

Grace sighs, "bits and pieces. But sometimes she talks about things that no one can decipher. Events that never happened."

Immediately after she quiets, a few more people share their own experiences as well, multiple family members having the same issues. By the time everyone is done, E is biting his bottom lip, focusing on the ground.

And then, almost as if he was never here at all, he gets up and leaves. He says nothing, not even the slightest goodbye or thank you. E doesn't even give anyone one last glance.

No one tries to stop him.

Chapter 10

The meeting ended shortly after E left. Everyone was silent, scared, I presume. I didn't even get to speak to Tyl before he left, whispering to Grace as they walked away in the same direction. Grey went to see Cora, and Lara went back to her house. So now I'm stuck, walking alone, thinking about everything that was said.

The founders of Petrichor, whoever they were, are the main cause of why the old world was destroyed.

They played victim and hero so that they could take power, taking everything away that they didn't deem fit.

They promised us the world was better. They *made* the world better, but did they truly? At what cost, exactly?

Is any of what E said actually true?

My thoughts continue to spiral as I catch something move out of the corner of my eye.

At first, my mind immediately assumes it's E, as he continues to pop up in situations similar to this one. Especially because it is a person, walking the same pace as me, glancing just like I am. However, even though I can't tell much about their appearance I can tell they're not E. Their head is shaved.

I begin to walk a bit faster, paranoia creeping up on me, and the person does the same.

Suddenly I'm wishing I wasn't a bus ride away from home. I'm wishing a lot of things. I'm almost wishing that it actually was E, as opposed to a stranger. A stranger that I know is looking at me. Always looking.

Luckily, for my sanity, they practically disappear the second I open the station doors.

The bus ride was normal. The walk home was normal. But, now that I'm home, I don't know what to do with myself. Typically, I would read whatever book I could get my hands on or watch whatever stupid movie was on our screen in the living room.

The screen where we don't get to choose what's on it. We can only turn it off and on. The screen that only shows movies that Petrichor allows.

With that in mind, suddenly, I can't do anything. I'm stuck deciding whether or not I believe E and what he said, or I go on with my normal life. If I don't look too deeply into things, I likely would never notice them. I would never notice what's allowed and what's not allowed. I would be happy, but I would also be ignorant.

I can't be ignorant, but I also don't have the mental capacity at the moment to truly dissect my life, and my bed just looks so inviting.

⁂

If it wasn't for Grey and Lara practically slamming down my front door, I think I would have slept all the way through the night.

"I want to see the shed!"

"What?" I ask groggily, opening the door fully to let them both in.

"I mentioned the shed to Lara that I showed you," Grey says to me then collapses onto the grey couch on which he's fallen asleep multiple times; "which obviously was a mistake. Since when do you care about old music, Lara? You seem perfectly fine with the current songs."

"I'm just curious. Nothing new happens anymore, besides the memory loss shit I guess, but that's just scary," she shrugs, "This sounds fun."

I smile a bit, "I wanted to take pictures of it at some point anyways, I guess we can go."

The idea has been in my head for days.

By the time we enter the street, Lara is still asking questions. I'm surprised by her enthusiasm; I would have expected her to chastise us instead. In a nice way. Maybe.

"How did you find it?"

Grey rolls his eyes and head simultaneously, "I walked through the forest and heard it. That's literally it, Lara."

"Huh."

I start to walk more quickly, not caring if they're following me. Grey knows where it is, he won't get lost. Anyways, I like this walk. It feels almost like a dream, or a past memory. That shed is sort of like a beacon of hope. Hope that one day maybe some questions will be answered. Things have been feeling off for a while now. I haven't wanted to admit it. Maybe it's because I've been with conspirators recently, if you can call them that, or because my parents are still gone.

"Meira."

A flashing green light reflects across my face.

Lara catches up to me, tilting her head up towards The Pass. I always like it when it's in use. The last couple of times, it was completely empty.

We're all still, trying to stay as quiet as possible. I can hear a car pull up behind us, quickly shutting off their headlights. We watch as a herd of deer slowly walk across the grass bridge above the road, forest to forest. They don't seem to notice us, nor do they even seem real.

I don't know how Petrichor did it. They built these over every road that needed them, any road that had the chance to harm wildlife. The

Pass is just one example of new architecture that makes this world so much different than the old one. Better. I like to believe that Mother Nature is proud of us now. Not scared, not miserable, but forever at peace. But maybe it was already too late for that.

Finally, the lights cease as we move to the side of the road. I squint my eyes, looking between the tree line. The creatures are nowhere to be seen.

"Let's go," I whisper, the sun beginning to cast a golden hue. I hope that the picture comes out with this lighting, it would look amazing.

Grey notices my increase in speed and groans, "We should be able to get there in time."

I like to be safe.

Just in case.

He was right, though, it only takes us about six minutes.

I swallow, taking in the scene. It's almost like a daze. The leaves sway softly, mirroring the movement of the wind chime as it plays mellow notes. The moss on the sides of the wood looks darker than the wood itself, like tiny living shadows taking their final rest.

"Are we almost there? We should speed up if—"

I turn to Lara, pointing towards the building.

"What?"

"This is it." I answer.

"What is it?"

Grey points wildly, "The shed, dumbass. What do you mean?"

"Where?"

"Lara, it's right there," he locks his concerned eyes on hers.

"You two are fucking with me."

"Lara . . ."

I exhale. Either she's extremely unobservant, which she's not, or she's joking with us.

Her eyes tell me that I'm wrong; there's no hint of comedy. Only confusion.

Something in the air causes tension to rise. We've been friends forever; we know when the other is joking. Something else is happening, and the slowly fading sunlight isn't helping either.

"Did you drink today?"

"Grey, I'm not fucking intoxicated. There's nothing there."

"Stop it."

"Stop what? Why would I lie about this?"

As anger flashes in her eyes I point to the wind chime, "Can you hear that?"

"Meira, I swear to fucking god if you're joking with me—"

"The wind chime?"

She shakes her head.

"We're leaving," Grey whispers. "Fuck this."

"I'm not—"

"I know you're not lying, that's the problem. We weren't supposed to see this, no way. Whatever this is, we're not supposed to be here."

I aim the camera at the shed, specifically the door, my hands shaking. *Please be there. Please, please be there.*

The camera clicks as the wind begins to stall. I run a hand through my hair, hesitating to look at the viewfinder.

My hands won't stop shaking. I can hear my blood rushing in my cars.

This is wrong.

"We need to go." My voice is small, raspiness caused by dread.

"Ira?"

I flip the camera towards them.

"Ira?" he raises his voice.

"It's not in the picture Grey."

I breathe.

"There's nothing there."

Chapter Eleven

March 30, 2073

7:30 PM

We need to go.

God, we need to go.

But we're rooted to the ground.

"You two swear?"

Grey and I don't even have to answer, she can tell by our eyes. Eyes which are still glued to the small screen of the camera. The screen that only shows trees, not the shed. The shed that seems to not exist.

Wonderful.

I flinch as the wind chime sounds again.

"Lara, please tell me you can hear that now," Grey pleads. She shakes her head.

He crouches close to the ground, "What the shit! We need to bring someone else out here."

"Cora?" I whisper, looking down at him.

"Let's try something first." Lara points shakily towards the building, "It's that way?"

She begins to walk, treading lightly. Metaphorically and literally. This place always felt different, but I thought it was all in my head. It's not, obviously. The air feels different, almost dirty. The more conscious I become of it, the harder it is to breathe.

There's something bigger happening here. Something that I don't want to uncover.

Yet, part of me does.

"How much farther?"

"A couple feet, reach out your arm," Grey answers, now fully sitting.

My breath hitches as her hand barely grazes the wall. She takes a step back, her shoulders rising and falling.

"Holy shit, I can feel it," Lara turns back around, her eyes wild. "We need to get Cora."

"They're with Tyl. Let's go."

"Wait," I hold Grey's shoulder so he remains on the ground instead of running off, "I don't know, shouldn't we alert the Emergency Line or something before going to get Cora?!"

I feel like I'm thinking logically, at least, as much as I can be considering the issue we're facing here. The Emergency Line of Petrichor handles things like . . . emergencies, obviously. Isn't that what this is? Seems like it to me.

Lara and Grey didn't seem to think so.

"No!" Both of my friends shout in unison.

I raise my hands in surrender as Grey attempts to stand.

Apparently, whoever is in there, if there's someone in there, does not want us to leave. A soft hissing sound starts around us, specifically in the trees. It grows louder as dark smoke winds between the grooves of the tree bark, slowly entering the air. I help Grey as he struggles to his feet, silently communicating our fear.

He keeps a firm hold on my hand, "Lara?"

She drops to the ground.

I try to run towards her, but Grey pulls me down with him. The smoke seems to gravitate and wrap around them, acting as a sort of soft blanket.

I'm not allowing myself to think.

I can't.

My body is numb with fear as I attempt to shake him conscious.

"Grey? Grey, you have to get up, we have to go . . ."

Nothing.

The black puffs bounce off me like they're hitting some sort of shield.

Grey's eyes flutter shut as his grip loosens. I run over to Lara, attempting to pull her closer to him, thinking that maybe moving her would help break whatever the hell this is. Her finger lightly twitches between mine.

She's breathing.

Thank god she's breathing.

But she won't move.

"Lara, hey, Lara, please . . . this isn't funny, please I—"

I glance back towards the way we came. No smoke. It's making an invisible wall of sorts, refusing to float past it. The only solution I can come up with is getting them past that wall so whatever the hell this smoke is can't affect them. I just hope I'm being logical. I just hope it isn't permanent.

I breathe in deeply, my whole body shaking. Whether it's fear or exhaustion, I'm not sure. Turning my back to the shed, I grab Lara under her arms, praying that this'll work.

It doesn't. She's completely limp, and I don't even think I can attempt to move Grey.

I'm forced to drop her as slowly as I can.

I stare at both of them. I can't just leave them. I can't.

I don't know what to do. Tears form in my eyes from both frustration and fear, why do I have to be the one unaffected by whatever is lingering in the air?

Why is it only me?

Distracting me instantly from my thoughts, a sharp pain erupts from my shoulder, rippling throughout my entire body.

My vision disappears in smoke.

Chapter Twelve

March 30, 2073

8:30 PM

The blood drips down my back.

"This isn't like you," she whimpers.

I sigh as she slowly slides the small blade out of my shoulder. The blood begins to flow even faster.

"I needed to feel it."

"Blood? Why?" she asks.

I don't need to nod; she knows the answer.

"I don't like hurting you."

I gently move closer to her, she's breaking inside.

It's my fault.

I know that.

But yet, I can't stop.

Her hand slips into mine, the blood dripping into my palm. I begin at her finger, leaving a train of kisses up her wrist, her arm, her shoulder, her neck. She releases a small sigh.

I stop at her ear, "I'm so sorry."

She tilts my head so I have to look into her eyes. I don't know whether to be scared or terrified of them. Scared about what she thinks of me; terrified to think about the chance she'll never look at me the same.

"I love you."

White flashes across my vision.

"You what?" I whisper.

She doesn't respond.

I stand up and walk to the bathroom, grabbing a towel quickly. I know she'll break if she has to stare at what she's done for too long.

I hand her the towel but she refuses to look up from examining her hand.

"What is it?"

"Why won't you tell me?"

She's talking about my blood . . . the blood that is so different from hers.

"It should be red," she mutters, "not—"

I cut her off, "Grey. It shouldn't be grey."

I've heard so many people say it. She finally takes the towel and wraps it around her hand, getting up to leave.

I grab her arm, "I love you too."

A tear falls down her cheek and rests on her top lip. I lean in, grasping the back of her head. Sometimes I wish she would bite my lip, cut me. Draw blood. Have it drip down my mouth, my neck, my chest.

"I can't," she takes a breath and backs away from me, "I'm not doing it anymore."

I'm too distracted to listen, staring at her lips but not her words.

"I'm done."

I snap into reality, "What?"

She runs her hand across my chest before she speaks, "You're beautiful."

I close my eyes.

"And you're here. You don't need your blood to remind you of that."

The color drains from my face. She knows.

Fuck.

She knows.

She knows why.

"Get out."

"I'm not dealing with this again . . . I can't lose you for weeks like last time. You're here, my love, you're real."

I only hear my thoughts. My thoughts tell me that I can't look at her, that she's dead to me. I run my fingers through my hair frantically as I clench my fists. Her voice is like a soft echo in my ear.

I need to feel it. Blood. Anyway I can. I do not feel real without it. Without it, I'm stuck in that place. That awful . . . I feel my skin boil as small cuts develop everywhere on my body. My blood starts to spill out of them, making a small puddle below me. The pain is overwhelming, the warmth enveloping. My mouth opens, screaming as I move towards the corner. I rest my head on the wall and cover my ears as the liquid pours out of them.

Then I feel her touching me. How is she not breaking . . . seeing what I did? I look down at my body, it doesn't even look real. How am I not dead?

Before I know it, she's in my arms.

". . . I-I'm sorry," is all I can manage.

I hold her as tightly as possible. I try to make her feel safe, protected, loved. She's sobbing against my chest as I move us slowly towards the floor. She's covered in my blood like a blanket.

"I'm here. It's still me. Please know that it's still me."

I love her . . . and I need her . . . why do I do this?

Her crying slows as she moves to look into my eyes. She puts her hand on my cheek.

"You stopped."

I nod, "It's done."

"Do I have—"

"You don't have to anymore," I whisper.

She smiles slowly.

That smile.

I fall for her every time.

I pull her closer, feeling her warmth. I doze off . . . and I believe she does too.

⁘

"Ira?"

No.

I'll pass.

I'm perfectly fine staying right here. I'm comfortable if I'm being honest. I'd rather not wake up. Not after that dream, nightmare, whatever it was. I can almost still feel the grey blood all over my body.

I should never have thought I was getting better. That whatever was causing the pain in my arm and in my head was nothing to worry about it.

Because it's back. Not only back, but worse. So much worse.

"Personally, I vote to leave. Not worth it. Someone will find her."

Thank you, unknown voice. I appreciate that, assuming he's talking about me.

"Hey, E, can you do us a favor and shut the fuck up? We're not leaving her."

Lara. That was definitely Lara.

E is here too, somehow.

Great.

He clears his throat; I can almost picture the exact expression on his face. Glee, only because he got a rise out of someone.

I can't leave them alone together, even if Grey is here too.

Blinking, I attempt to move. Nothing. It takes all of my strength to squint my eyes, the sunlight like a razor. Pain leaks into my mind as I hear the people around me start to notice. I can't even see them, only the trees. The trees are good company at the moment. Quiet, not arguing, not some stranger who thinks he knows everything, only the familiar trees.

And now E.

"She's fine, unfortunately," he states, then lowers his voice just enough to where the rest of the group would still hear, "I thought you would have at least had some cuts and bruises, angel, it would have actually made you somewhat interesting."

Asshole

"Yeah," I cough, "that's my goal in life, for you to find me interesting."

E smirks before standing out of his crouch above me.

Another figure settles me against their chest.

Grey is here. Good.

"Before you ask what happened, we have no clue. Black smoke made us all fucking collapse, that's it. We went to get Cora and Tyl after we woke up. They'll be here soon," Lara says from behind me.

E clicks his tongue, "so you left your helpless friend here knocked out cold while you went to find that arrogant child? Good friends, the both of you, truly."

If he wasn't himself, and if the whole point of that question wasn't to attack everyone in the situation, it almost would have sounded like he was coming to my defense. But he wasn't, and I couldn't care less.

"It wasn't like that," Grey starts, his voice vibrating against the back of my neck, "we woke up a couple feet away, outside of the smoke. We didn't see her, so we assumed she went to find help. Obviously, we were wrong. Neither of us could message Cora or Tyl, so we had to go."

I don't know when I had passed out, or how I ended up so far away from Grey and Lara, another unknown to add to my list.

"You never thought that, perhaps, she was *inside* of the smoke? Or is that just too complicated for you?" E questions.

I already know Lara is not going to let that slide. Perhaps I wouldn't either if this was a normal situation, if I didn't have a splitting headache.

"Do you ever shut up? No one is listening to you anyways; we don't want to hear you speak just because you like the sound of your own voice." Lara spits back.

E straightens the bottom of his black sweater, an amused grin on his face. He's enjoying this.

Of course he is.

I dig my fingers into the pine straw, trying to stretch my aching joints. I really need to stand up.

Using Grey's shoulder as support, I slowly hoist myself up. My eyes still aren't fully adjusted, but they're clear enough to see my surroundings. Clear enough to see the person staring back at me.

"Why are *you* here?"

I didn't mean for my tone to be harsh, but I don't want to take it back. If everyone else is talking to him like that, I can too. Like I said, he's easy for me to read. If he ever seems to truly feel hurt because of my words, I think I would be able to tell.

At the moment, however, there's zero hurt. Only sheer malice and enjoyment.

"Walking in the woods, saw these two holding a body on the ground," he nods towards my friends, "got interested, saw you dead, got more interested."

I press my lips together, deciding to attempt a nonchalant reaction.

"Ira being knocked out on the ground is entertainment to you?" Grey stands, still holding onto my swaying form.

E ignores him, "Let me see the camera."

"My camera? You know about the picture?"

"Lara enlightened him," Grey answers, "after we found the camera almost shattered on the ground."

My voice lessens, "Shattered?"

"Yes, very—"

"It's just cracked," Lara cuts E off.

She reaches under her jacket to hand it to me. I run my finger over the crack, my emotions too crazed to even care. Maybe I can get it fixed.

"May I?" E asks gently, moving slightly closer.

His voice causes my ears to ring. I stare at him incredulously, surprised by the gentleness in his eyes. Before I can interject, E snatches the camera from my hand. I shouldn't have trusted that supposed innocence.

"Give it back to her-"Lara demands.

"Ah," E raises a finger towards Lara's face, "not yet."

She scowls, forming her hands into fists at her side.

E raises the camera, pointing it directly towards the shed.

"You can see it too?" Grey whispers.

"No, I'm just a fucking psychic."

He really could have just said yes.

E snaps a picture, knowing how to use my camera perfectly. Real cameras barely even exist anymore; I'm lucky to have mine.

"How do you know how to use that?" Lara asks, her thoughts matching my own. E chooses not to respond again, running his thumb across the buttons. My eyes switch from my camera to his hand. Scarred. I blink, staring back down; it isn't a small scratch to say the least.

"Interesting," he whispers.

"Believe me now, asshole?" Lara questions.

E shrugs, "Needed proof first."

Lara takes a long sigh as I rest my head gently against the crook of Grey's neck. He smells earthy, a mix of lavender and oak.

"Meira! Are you okay?"

Grey turns abruptly, taking me with him. I wince at the whiplash. He smooths my hair back, a silent apology to combat the throbbing pain in my neck. However, a small smile does appear on my face as Tyl appears. He looks slightly more ashen than last time.

"Are you okay?" he repeats as he gets closer.

I nod, realizing that I forgot to respond, "I'm okay . . . thank you."

"Cora's behind a little bit." Tyl motions towards me. "I can take her if you want to explain to them what happened."

Grey nods, handing me off gently to Tyl. He holds on to my arm with his left hand, stabilizing my lower back with his right.

"I'm going to look around the back of the building, see if any-thing's there," E says, shifting his feet uncomfortably. It almost makes me want to laugh. Seeing E do relatively normal things immediately seems out of character for him. I mean, it's close to impossible to even imagine him sleeping. Based on the purple splotches under his eyes, though, I don't think he does. It takes a large portion of my energy to even remember that he's human.

Lara gives him a fake grin, "You do that. Try to get lost while you're at it."

He surprisingly doesn't make a smart comment back, instead disappearing around the wall.

Thank God.

"Why's he here?" Tyl whispers into my ear.

I shrug lightly, "He says he was just walking through the woods and saw us."

"He's bad at making up excuses."

Tyl is right, it does sound like an excuse. Personally, I don't think he knows many people. It doesn't seem like it, at least, espe-cially because we've never seen him before. If even Grey and Lara don't know who you are, you don't get out much. I think he's bored. Lonely, maybe. Makes me almost feel bad for him.

Almost.

"Tyl?"

Cora's voice sounds from the trees as Grey immediately begins to move towards it. I watch as he hugs them briefly, whispering. I'm glad no one else had to explain this to Cora, it would take too long if it was me. Grey's good at summarizing. Lara would over exaggerate, if it's even possible to do that in this situation.

"So I finally get to meet this E person? I'm excited."

"Don't be," Lara responds as Cora arrives and nods my way.

"Glad you're okay."

"Thank you," I whisper.

Tyl leans his head down on mine and I remain still. It's comforting, I'll admit. The tension in my shoulders loosens as I avoid eye contact with Lara and Grey. They're probably smiling. communicating silent jokes between each other. Out of mind, out of sight.

"Where is he?" Cora asks.

I answer too fast, "Behind the shed."

Tyl lifts his head as I mentally chastise myself.

Damn it.

He didn't have to move.

I appreciated the small amount of contact. Of peace.

I look up at him, curly blonde hair gracefully blowing in the wind. Just like a movie. Just like Apollo.

"Can you see it . . . the building?"

Cora and Tyl both shake their heads.

"When Grey came to find me, he said that the camera couldn't pick it up either. Can I see?" Tyl asks the group.

Grey glances at me as Lara strains her neck towards the sky.

"It's with Mr. People Pleaser," Lara frowns and tilts her eyes past me, "the same one who didn't listen to me when I told him to get lost."

I whip my head to follow her gaze.

Shit. Ow.

I really need to stop doing that.

E is standing close to the building, hands tucked into the pockets of a long black coat. Did he have that the whole time? Maybe he did, I can't remember. He holds a blank stare almost as if he's trying to seem melancholy, but his eyes tell a different story. I have to look away.

Tyl straightens, "Cora, this is E. E, this is Cora."

The wind chime sounds suddenly, almost as a silent warning that only half of us can hear.

I don't think I've ever seen someone look like the embodiment of shock before this moment. The moment they laid eyes upon E, Cora's face became ghostly pale. Their mouth is opened slightly, eyes flickering between emotions every second. I've seen a video before of one of those old gambling machines, the ones where you try to get the spinning pictures to match up so you can win money. That is exactly what Cora's eyes look like, and the final spin lands finally on desperate anger.

After many painfully long seconds of pure silence, they run their hand roughly through their hair, "What does E stand for?"

Weird question.

I reluctantly switch my gaze towards E, who looks the exact opposite. No emotions, face taut, eyes blank. A mask, I assume. Assessing.

"My name."

A small grin penetrates through his facade.

Rude comment.

Bad timing.

"Which—"

Cora takes a step closer to him.

"Is—"

Another step

"—what?"

One final step.

E cracks a fully pained smile, "You know my name, Cora, there's no need to test me. Unless, of course, it would fuel whichever sadistic side of your brain controls your actions."

The rest of us remain silent; this is something beyond us. All I can hope for at the moment is an eventual explanation for the murder in both pairs of eyes.

"You should have played dumb," Cora continues to move closer, taking something out of their pocket, "I would have bought it. I'm surprised you even decided to . . . *keep* any and all parts of yourself."

I can tell that they're choosing their words carefully. For who's sake, I don't know.

I'm thinking I don't know anything anymore.

E reaches for his pocket as well, "it would all be gone if I had it my way."

I realize what they're both holding when a flash of metal catches in the light. They're knives.

And not just kitchen knives.

Those are daggers, a rarity to find in today's society.

Not only that, but they're electric, somehow. Every time they shift the blades in their grasps, a thin strip of pulsating white light along the blades responds back.

Tyl notices at the same moment I do, "Wait!"

E suddenly points the end of the blade towards Tyl and I, "Please enlighten us on what exactly you would like to add to this situation? Whatever it is, I bet we couldn't continue without it."

Tyl doesn't move.

"You fucker. Why are you acting like this?" Cora points their knife at E.

"Like what, exactly? Lovely, patient, charming? I'm sure there's a long list of words used to describe me."

I can only assume he means us.

"I can see now the reason they explained you as they did, but I never expected it. You never even crossed my mind when Grey told me about E."

He clenches his jaw, absently running his forefinger across the handle, "a shame."

Cora examines his face, that feigned calm. But, unlike us, they seem to notice something deeper.

"It was you, wasn't it? You finally abandoned your stupid fucking philosophy and did it, didn't you?"

E's eyes light up like flames. The mask is gone.

"You shouldn't be angry, you already planned on doing it without my knowledge," he mockingly answers.

Before E could react, Cora lunges forward and forces him against a tree, holding his neck at knifepoint. The white glow begins to change to red.

"Cora?" Grey's voice cuts through the tension.

They ignore him.

"Admit it. I wanna hear you fucking admit it."

"Or my neck ends up like my hand?" E counters.

Cora hesitates, "Depends."

"Do it then," he runs his tongue across his teeth. "Do it. Even if you didn't finish the job, you would be doing me a favor."

They whisper something close to his ear, inaudible. E's face suddenly softens as his eyes snap shut.

"You forget who else was there."

Cora presses the blade deeper, which only causes E's grin to grow wider and the red light to grow brighter, "I know damn well who was there."

"Then I'll say this one more time, use your fucking brain," he whispers slowly, his eyes burning with a passion I've never seen anyone have before, "if it wasn't me and it wasn't you, then who the fuck do you think did it, Cora?"

They drop the knife and the light shuts off immediately, "What?"

"You heard me."

"But she wasn't supposed to . . ."

"You took that risk when you decided to bring her; I had to clean up your mess. I made my choice after it was all over." E slowly puts his blade back in his pocket.

"There wouldn't even be a mess in the first place if—"

"Hey guys, I'm sorry to interrupt . . . but what the fuck is going on?"

Lara.

Thank you.

"Nothing," Cora sniffs, returning to take their spot next to Grey. "I just didn't think I would see this piece-of-shit today, or ever, for that matter."

"Nope, we're not doing that. What just happened was a whole lot more than nothing," Lara bends to pick up Cora's blade. "I mean, hell, you were gonna kill him. Why'd you stop?"

I wait to see the light appear when she grabs it off the ground, but it doesn't, not until it's put back into Cora's hand. I think I'm the only one that noticed.

"Very good question," Tyl finally speaks up.

E walks back towards us, the knife reappearing in his hand, "I mean, if anyone wants to try then go straight ahead. Like I said, human nature."

Cora scoffs and whispers something under their breath.

Tyl pulls me closer to him, but I barely notice. I'm fully focused on the hilt of the blade. Blood red.

A voice crawls out from the deepest parts of my mind.

Sometimes I wish she would bite my lip, cut me. Draw blood.

I push it back; it doesn't matter right now. I blink in an attempt to readjust myself. To focus on the moment. Breathe.

E glances at me before returning back to Cora. They follow his gaze.

Cora's eyes narrow, "Don't, you know the risks."

E's mouth twitches into a malicious smile, "Oh, but it would be so fun."

"Don't what?"

Grey finally cuts through the conversation, sadness and confusion plastering his face.

"There are some things that I'm not ready to talk about," Cora grazes Grey's arm gently, "I just wanted to make sure that E understands that."

"You have no idea," E scoffs.

"Fine, if you two are done here then, we have shit to do."

I agree with Lara. Whatever just happened is obviously still an open wound. Even though my curiosity is yelling at me, I know I shouldn't ask. Maybe eventually they'll tell us. All I know is that they have hatred that runs deeper than even the pain in my head at the moment.

"Right," Cora swallows, "Can I see the camera?"

E walks up to them, setting my camera in their outstretched hand.

"You look old, Cora."

"You need a haircut, little brother."

Chapter Thirteen

March 30, 2073

9:00 PM

Siblings.

That complicates things.

Cora and E.

Izmene.

Family.

God, what I would do for those genes.

"You can't be serious," Tyl whispers, letting out an exasperated sigh. Even with the sun almost completely drowned in the horizon, I can still see the look on Tyl's face. The disappointment.

I think he believed E would be a temporary figure—or at least hoped.

We all did.

Partly.

With what we just learned, though, it seems like he's here to stay.

Shit.

I look between the two of them as I make mental connections. Yeah, it makes sense. Same jawline, similar noses, same grins, opposite hair. Siblings.

Of course.

"Little brother? Like an actual brother, or like, metaphorically?"

E feigns a smile, "Cora and I share the same blood, Grey, if that helps define the term."

"I still don't understand how you two can be from the same parents . . . they must have been in a horrible sex position when they conceived you, E," Lara scowls.

"Probably," Cora mumbles, examining the picture on the camera, "Well, fuck," Grey whines, "I mean, you told me you had a brother but I never expected it to be this son of a—"

"I'm pleasantly surprised you even told people about me, Cora. I, for one, would have much preferred to be an only child. I assumed you felt the same."

"Well, they also said they hated you," Grey adds.

Cora hands the camera back to me, "Bingo."

I reluctantly move away from Tyl to walk towards the shed. I hear him shift his feet behind me, cracking his knuckles. Placing my hand on the outside wall, I wave Cora over with my other, E observing every movement.

They place their hand next to mine.

"Weird," Cora whispers.

"I'm sorry he's your brother," is all I can manage. Might be an odd statement, but the sentiment is there. Somewhere

"Thank you," they chuckle. "He didn't used to be like this."

"Hard to believe."

A brief pause.

"I know."

"What changed?" I whisper.

I can see their eyes shift to solemn in the growing darkness.

There was still some part, likely as deep as they could bury it, that still cared about their brother. Even after whatever happened between them.

They sigh, "He had to grow up."

Tyl appears next to me, oblivious to two people talking privately. He runs his hand along the wood panels.

"This has to be Petrichor."

"Who else?" Cora agrees. "What does it look like?"

"Extremely run down, like a shed from before the end."

I can see Tyl visibly swallow.

"Before," he repeats.

I nod.

"Can we get inside?" Lara joins the line, purposefully shoving E away from us and he raises his hands in a mock surrender. Her hostility is inspiring.

Sometimes I wonder whether or not she has a full murder plan for everyone she hates. I mean, she knows how to fight. Lara's parents are two of the strongest people I've ever seen, mentally and physically. She has an older brother as well, but as she states, he's better off forgotten. All Lara has practically ever said about him was how strong his pride was, and I could see where he got it from. He left a long time ago to go back to Korea, then decided never to return. Her brother promised he would, but she believes he found wealth and was too selfish to even call. The family barely speaks about him anymore.

I sometimes wonder if he's okay. I know Lara does too.

"I don't think we should," Tyl finally answers. "We already know it's not safe. I think we should reconvene somewhere, try to find information about it. I have room at my place if we want to go there and also I have," he takes a sharp breath, "something else that might be better to speak about later."

I don't know if there really is a reason for Tyl's secrecy, or if he's trying to prove the importance of whatever he's talking about.

"God, the dramatics. It's a shame you decided to pursue . . . whatever this is as opposed to theater."

We all spin around unanimously. E turns his attention to the sky above, tucking his hair behind his ears.

"That was really funny, maybe you should have pursued being a fucking comedian," Grey feigns a laugh as he starts to walk back towards the street. Glancing up at Tyl, a wave of pity washes over me. His eyes remain neutral but yet I can see the urge to comment back in the way he fidgets with his fingers.

I attempt to distract him, "Is your place okay?"

He nods, shooting me a small smile. Cora notices my attempt and adds, looking directly at him, that E won't be joining us. That was then followed by an upstanding agreement, much to E's amusement.

"That's fine then, leave, as long as you're at peace with losing information, as well as outstanding advice."

Lara clicks her tongue, "you know, E, you keep saying that but all that's come out of your mouth so far has been shit."

He takes a quick breath, bending low to pick up a stick from the forest floor.

"I bet the one up your ass looks just like that," Cora bristles.

E points it at them, a fake frown plastered on his face, "Good one, really, that was impressive."

I roll my eyes. He's extremely hard to deal with, I know this, but yet sometimes I feel a bit of envy. Being quick-witted isn't easy to come by, especially in a society where there aren't a million things to complain about. My parents have told stories before about my comedy when I was younger, so I guess maybe I used to have that skill. When I think back, though, I can't come up with any specific examples. Neither can my parents. Maybe it's better that no one remembers; they have nothing to compare the current me to.

"You like photography? Cameras?"

I stare at him, unable to hide my urge to answer. He quirks an eyebrow as he raises the stick up to a tree. Nodding, I allow my gaze to follow the point to a small hole perfectly disguised.

"Camera," he smooths his hair back, "many of them, actually. See?"

Before any of us can respond, E begins to walk from tree to tree, pointing out many supposed cameras. They don't look like cameras.

I've seen cameras.

They definitely don't look like cameras.

I slowly walk closer to one about my height, shamefully interested. This place has obviously turned out to be dangerous, and yet here I am, somehow wanting to stay. Part of my brain is screaming at me to leave it alone, and a couple days ago I most likely would have.

But now something's different and I feel more reckless; it's scary but it's also somehow freeing. It's new.

And then it moves.

The hole in the tree just . . . *moves*.

I tilt my head to the side. The small, now noticeable, grey lens also moves to the side. I tilt my head to the other side. The lens tilts to the other side. It's actually kind of cute. "Why do you know this?" Cora interjects, their voice smooth.

"Observation."

Always observing.

"Dear God," Tyl rubs the bridge of his nose, "We're supposed to believe that? You somehow just observed these cameras that, standing right next to them, we didn't even see?"

My gaze returns to the lens as it zooms slightly in and out, attempting to focus.

"I come here a lot . . . the music caught my attention. Real music, not whatever the fuck was playing at that party. If you come here enough times then eventually you notice when man-made eyes are staring at you, no matter how small."

His eyes cut to me.

"Music?" Tyl asks.

I open my mouth to speak but Grey beats me to it, "Let's go to your place before we talk more about it, we don't know what else is hidden."

"E, you're not coming," Cora demands.

"I feel as if I have every right to know about this place, as well as whatever information *he* says he holds," E points to Tyl, "especially as I'm now a member of Ignite, I suppose? Give me a reason why I shouldn't go."

"For one, we don't know you. We don't know legitimately anything about you, you just showed up saying you have information for Tyl, and now you want to be a part of everything?"

Lara is right. There are too many mysteries.

"Let him come. We'll see what he has to say."

All of our eyes travel to Tyl, even E's.

Always the gentlemen. Allowing E to tag along, even despite how he treats him. Constantly. How he treats everyone.

"Fine," Cora shoots their sibling a look of disgust, "let's go."

Chapter 13

Lara shoots a concerned look my way, raising a thumbs up in question. At least I can read that signal easily, she gives it a lot. I raise my thumb as well, communicating that I'm able to walk fine—hopefully. Did she and Grey also feel like this when they woke up? I'm not sure how long they were awake before I was, but it doesn't seem like they had any trouble. It doesn't seem like their right arms are in scorching pain or their brains feel like they're melting.

All good signs, right?

Completely normal.

Everything is completely normal.

Chapter Fourteen

March 30, 2073

9:00 PM

Raleigh.

The same as it always was.

Petrichor never changed the names of cities; they said it was unnecessary. I mean, it wasn't the name's fault that the old cities failed. Petrichor filtered through history, deciding what to keep and what not to keep. Names and books. All kept. Movies, TV shows, and music? Not so much. Only a select few are still able to be found today, most of which are extremely uninteresting. I don't like thinking about it. All of the art we lost because of greed, all of the art I've never been able to see. My parents told me that these pieces of society were deemed unfit to stay because of the choices the old artists and directors were making. Things that used to be beautifully creative were turned into capitalistic monsters used to trick viewers into buying, selling, or whatever else the creators wanted. Movies were barely movies anymore; art pieces were barely art pieces. Just profit. Pure, selfish profit. Even music took the same route as the other arts. Songs about buying this product, songs about buying that product, songs about how the earth wasn't dying and how everything would be okay. The earth, on the contrary, was in fact dying. But who would buy anything if they thought they were going to die before they could enjoy it? Exactly. Monsters.

Anything that even had a minor factor in humanity's eventual downfall, Petrichor did not want it anymore.

God, I could rant about this for hours.

There was only one saving grace. Books. Books never followed suit. Back then they were considered "outdated" and were never used as a capitalistic medium. Because of this, Petrichor made sure that as many books as possible were saved. See, Petrichor never went out of their way to destroy any movies or music during the "almost-fall" of the earth, but they never went out of their way to save them either. Like I said before, music and movies aren't illegal . . . just extremely hard to find. Or so I thought, before meeting Izmene.

I scratch my cheek, realizing too late that I was intently staring at the sign on the wall that reads our destination. Raleigh, it states. Underneath it is a small promotion for a new movie, *We Had It Coming*. A bit harsh, but understandable. Describing today's movies would be very similar to describing today's music. Not even close to as bad as the ones made right before the fall, but not even close to as good as the real ones made when art and expression was still the main goal. Creative, yet boring. Not selfish, yet not exactly moving.

I really need to stop staring. I need to focus on now, on what just happened, but it feels like everything is trying to pull my attention away.

However, I'm not the only one.

Arms crossed tightly across his chest; E's gaze is on the sign as well. The metro door closes, blocking the point of interest, right as I move cautiously to sit down. The rest of the group does the same. I close my eyes, listening to the sound of the metro pick up quickly, moving us towards the heart of the city. A small gasp erupts from someone across from me and I can immediately assume where we are. There's a short section on this track that glides over a man-made lake, filled with perfectly clear water that was manufactured to keep the bioluminescent organisms that dwell in it safe. Even though darkness had fully taken over now, you can see the lake as clear as day because of them.

I've always loved it, but because the floor of the metro is clear, it almost feels like you're falling.

E, obviously, felt that too.

"Don't use this metro much?" Cora jeers.

"No," E twirls a piece of his hair, "I don't."

They snort, "Most people have to take this metro almost every day; what makes you the exception?"

A genuine question veiled in a harsh tone.

"I'm the exception to most things."

E stands, tongue pressed against his cheek, and moves to the empty seat next to me.

Away from Cora.

Why did they have to say something?

I was perfectly fine before I turned into the barrier between E and Cora. Everyone else is completely zoned out, Lara even has her eyes closed.

E begins to tap his foot impatiently and, simply because he's the one doing it, it's like nails on a chalkboard.

My voice sounds quietly before I can even catch myself, "please, stop."

He turns his head slowly and out of the corner of my eye I can see him analyzing me. Observing.

"You know, I've noticed you barely speak, but the rest of your friends don't seem to share the sentiment."

E's voice is even quieter than my own.

Breathe in.

Breathe out.

"Do you have any friends?"

It might be an honest question, but I meant it just how he took it.

"We're not friends then, angel? Truly, I'm hurt."

I'm just praying that no one is eavesdropping, especially when he keeps calling me—

"Why do you call me that?"

He blows out a breath and I finally meet his gaze, the corners of his mouth twitching into a grin, "So many questions tonight. Do you like when I call you that?"

I flick my eyes back to the floor, "You can't answer a question with another question."

"Says who?"

I shake my head. I don't have the energy for this.

"Fine then," E continues, practically whispering, "ask another, if you have one. Which, I assume you do, considering I'm so—"

"Why do you speak like that?"

It's something I've noticed from the beginning. He always chooses his words carefully; delicately strung together like he's been doing it for centuries.

"It's how I grew up, how I was taught. Cora too, but it seems as if they worked to erase it."

I steal one gaze away from the floor to look at Cora, their head resting on the wall behind them, eyes closed now as well.

Likely listening.

When I turn back, he's still staring.

"What?" I ask simply.

"Do you have a reason for these questions?"

Well. No, not really. Curiosity, maybe? Wanting to understand the origins of all of the hatred that laces every word he speaks, no matter who he's talking to. Because that's what it is. Hatred. Hatred in his eyes, hatred in the way he moves. Everything.

Everything.

I've never met someone like that before.

Someone who wasn't . . . content. Obviously, we all have our moments in which we dislike our lives, ourselves, but eventually, it goes away. It always goes away. Everyone around me becomes content again. I even become content again. Or, rather, *became*. I don't know if I'm content now or if I'm happy deep down.

It's different. It's new.

After a painful throb erupts from my temple and reminds me where I am, I lean my head on my hands, waiting to see if E continues the conversation.

Luckily, for my sanity, he doesn't.

Unluckily, it takes quite a long time for my mind to be able to peel away from the boy sitting beside me. But, eventually, I'm able to wonder how Grey is feeling right now. I don't even really know how I would be feeling. Probably not good. Definitely not good.

Why does it have to be E? Cora's *brother*.

Honestly, anyone else besides him would have certainly worked out better. Cora and Grey have a bond, one that I really thought was going to stick; but after this epiphany, I'm not sure. Obviously, it's out of Cora's control that they have a shit brother, but now Grey is stuck with him too.

I think we all are.

It's safe to assume that at this point, Grey hates him. Hates him for how he treats everyone, Tyl especially. Hates him for the unknown past that led to Cora's thoughts towards their own brother. We don't even know the full extent of those thoughts, and we probably don't want to. Well, that's not true.

We definitely want to.

Respectfully.

Who could blame us? Who wouldn't want to know the origins of a disposition that led to a knife fight with one's own sibling? No one. That's a moment that's only seen in books. Maybe movies too, I wouldn't really know. I've only seen a fight once in my life, a couple months ago while classes were still in session. There was a girl named Blaire, a year or two older than me, but about four inches shorter.

That's an important detail, I promise.

Anyways, she hated us. Just because it's a perfect world doesn't mean there aren't outliers. Blaire, in the nicest way of putting it, is the biggest outlier I've ever met. She believed it was her personal goal in life to state her vendetta against all of our dating lives. Which, mind you, she barely knew anything about besides the small-school talk that happens continuously.

Grey, according to her, was a slut.

Lara, according to her, was a hermit.

I, according to her, was a lost cause.

In other words, it would be a miracle if anyone would even want to have a relationship with me at all.

That one stung a bit, even from her. That comment is also the one that started the whole fiasco. The second it spilled from Blaire's lips, Grey immediately fired back, "You know, I can hear all of this shit coming out of your mouth but all I can question is why your boyfriend is cheating on you when you obviously," he motioned to the length of her body, "have the breath-taking skill of being able to remain standing whilst you give head?"

She slapped him. Lara punched her. A lot of blood. Grey pulled Lara away. That was the last time we spoke to Blaire.

What we do know though is that her boyfriend was in fact cheating on her.

With Grey!

In Lara and I's defense, we didn't know. Grey told us after the fight, but he did state that home-wrecking was against his moral code . . . except in this case.

Needless to say, Blaire and her boyfriend are broken up now.

Now look who's the lost cause.

"-not what I said."

I quickly turn my head, looking for the source. Two Petrichor workers walk alongside each other through the aisles of the metro as they laugh at some untold joke.

Great.

Everyone in the group stiffens almost at once, except for E and I. He seems completely unaware of the tension shift, remaining to stare down at the floor.

Eventually, the workers finally get close enough for him to take notice of the small logos on their shirts. Squinting, I follow his gaze. The letter "P," bolded and stitched onto the left side of their chest.

A small green leaf sprouts from the top, almost like a small plant. I always thought it was kind of cute, considering that I see it almost always on my parent's uniforms.

I'm used to it by now.

E, on the other hand, seems to be quite the opposite. He slouches quickly, beginning to play with a strand of hair in front of his face. Everyone else is doing similar things to appear natural.

I exhale, this is unnecessary. Assuming that everyone is tense due to the fact that we might have just found some sort of . . . secret, I guess? Which was—the shed.

Shit, the shed.

It feels like it's been days since we even left the forest, and even longer since we realized the shed was invisible to certain people. *Invisible.* I can't believe my mind even allowed me to not focus on that aspect for even a moment. How I was able to think about anything else is beyond me.

But, even so, I highly doubt there's any reason to worry.

Maybe.

The Petrichor workers seem too young to question us, and we don't even know what department they work for. Hell, they could be janitors for all we know.

Yet, that doesn't change the fact that their path is leading right towards us. Directly.

Maybe there is a reason to worry.

"We need a distraction," Cora whispers through gritted teeth.

"Do you think they know about the shed?" Tyl whispers back.

Even though all reason seems to point towards the fact that they likely don't know, once Tyl said it out loud, nausea starts to grow in my stomach.

Cora shrugs, nudging Grey and whispering something in his ear. He nods quickly as he begins one of the loudest coughing fits ever.

Quite a distraction.

I roll my eyes. Let's say the shed is owned by the government. How would they even know about our visit this quickly, let alone that we were the people there?

"The cameras," Lara whispers, likely to herself but loudly enough for all of us to panic.

The cameras. Silent eyes, seemingly watching our every move in the forest. Silent eyes that only E noticed.

"If you have any more random information about this whole situation," Tyl leans towards E, "We would much rather you explain sooner or later."

He doesn't answer, his gaze flicking between the oncoming workers and his sibling.

There's something like panic in E's eyes.

"We didn't do anything," I chime in, "Even if they did know we were there through those cameras, they won't do anything. At most they'll question us, but we stumbled upon it by accident. They can't blame us."

I mean, it's true, but even if everyone agrees with me, the uneasiness doesn't settle.

Tyl stays silent and stares down at the floor. Out of our whole group, he seems to be the most impacted by the appearance of these workers. Before I open my mouth to ask if he's alright, a thought slips into place.

Shit.

Ignite.

If Petrichor knows about Ignite, they most likely aren't incredibly fond of its leader. They would never go so far as to outlaw questioning groups such as Ignite, or I hope they wouldn't, but they still are indeed the ones being questioned. I doubt they would do anything harsh, but I understand the wish not to find out.

Unfortunately, Grey's coughing fit does nothing except cause the workers to take notice of us.

"Useless," E mutters under his breath.

Cora replies, raising their voice in the process, "Do you have something better? You wouldn't even speak a moment ago."

"Always," he grins while simultaneously turning towards me, "May I?"

"May you what?"

"Distract."

His tone is indifferent, but the twitching of his hand says otherwise. The way his shoe taps against the glass.

"What does that entail?" Tyl chimes in.

E completely ignores his question, staring at me for a response.

I eye the workers from my peripheral and their newfound interest in Grey's supposed sickness. Luckily for us, the other passengers stop them periodically, asking about this and that. "My wife is having issues again . . . her mind just isn't what it used to be. Her memory, especially, but I've heard others having the same issues and . . . I just want to make sure everything is okay . . . has Petrichor heard about this?" An older man rambles, straightening his brown cap.

One of the workers nods thoughtfully as the other replies, "I'm sorry sir, we don't have the authority to answer that question."

Sure.

They don't know the answer, in fancier terms.

Considering my current situation, I don't think I have the mental power to think deeper on what the man was saying.

The memory issues.

For another time, I promise myself.

I'll question it another time.

Unfortunately, that conversation was the last barrier between us and them, meaning that we barely have any choices now.

"Sure," I whisper desperately, "distract."

Before I can barely even finish the last word, one of E's hands slides around to cradle the back of my head. My eyes go wide as he places his other gently on my knee, leaning in, our faces only an inch apart. I have no choice but to match his gaze.

At this moment, I could be anything. I could be anyone. I have no idea what's happening or who I am. I have no idea why his eyes hold a pain so unmatched when he looks into mine. I have no idea why this moment seems to last forever or why there's something in my mind screaming at me not to look away.

Don't worry, I attempt to soothe myself.

I don't think I could look away if I wanted to.

E's hand has moved from my knee to my chin, slowly tilting his head to his right and mine to the left. Just the slightest bit closer and I might regret everything that I've ever been, or anything that I might become.

This isn't me.

This is someone else completely, or maybe they're one and the same.

Maybe we're one and the same.

He backs away before I can make that decision.

"Gone?"

"Gone," I repeat, not fully comprehending the question before answering. The two are in fact gone now, though, shoulders shaking in a light chuckle as they walk back towards the way they came.

To be honest, E was being smart. The workers were young enough to hate public displays of affection, and what just happened would likely have made anyone look away. Even me.

"I suppose," E leans forward to look at Tyl, "That you're now battling with the undeniable fact that you wish nothing more than to be me? I understand it's hard to see your dreams fall into another's hands."

Asshole.

Fucking asshole.

Whatever it was that just happened between E and I, it doesn't matter anymore. That didn't mean anything to him, and it didn't mean anything to me either.

I was lying to myself.

I was trying to conceptualize a perfect reality in which E is actually a decent human being with the ability to say anything meaningful.

Obviously, in this reality, that is extremely far from the truth.

"Touch her again and you're dead," Lara threatens, her face red hot with anger.

His grin only grows.

"Cora asked for a distraction, I distracted successfully. Are you okay?" E turns the question back towards me.

After a moment, I nod, searching for any hint of genuine concern in what he said. Maybe there was, maybe there wasn't, I couldn't really tell.

E refuses to meet my eyes even as he motions towards me, "see? If you're not going to listen to my words then at least listen to hers."

"Are you sure you're okay?" Tyl whispers close to my ear. I nod once more, shooting him a comforting smile. Cora has a look of death plastered across their face.

"I agreed, and it ended up working. No harm done," I assure him, loud enough for the rest of the group to hear as well.

No harm done.

True, yet my world is flipped upside down. Maybe I wasn't lying to myself.

Wasn't ignoring the pain thundering in my head.

The feeling of uncertainty deep in my blood.

E's hand is clutching the edge of his seat, his knuckles white.

***

The walk was short after we got off the metro, providing just enough time for E to say absolutely nothing. The only addition he provided to the journey was some death stares aimed towards Tyl and I. Cora walked only two paces behind him, fidgeting with something hidden within their pocket. The knife, I assume. Making sure that E didn't try anything.

Makes sense, I fully expect someone to be bloodily murdered at E's hands by the end of whatever expedition we're going on. Not Tyl though, I believe that E is too intimidated by him. Too intimidated by the respect he gains from anyone he talks to, too intimidated by the charm in Tyl's voice that could only be gained through intelligence. E has that intelligence, but not that same type of charm. He might have charm, but it's fueled by hatred. Hatred for something unknown.

Hatred, perhaps, for the world we're living in.

Every second he swivels his head and deeply examines the buildings we pass by. He's not impressed, I can tell by the small sighs from him moment to moment. To be honest, I don't understand it. The city is like an impossible dream, yet proven to be incredibly possible. Buildings grow tall instead of wide with walls completely built in glass. Vines and different native plants somehow were planted to thrive on these walls, covering the windows that the residents would like to keep private. Some are even moved to hook into bundles which allow for natural light to be let into the lofts. Again, a perfect balance between nature and machine. There are no roads in sight besides the small paved paths used for service vehicles. Maintenance, deliveries, emergencies, what have you. Cars are outlawed in cities, which means the only way to get to your destination would be walking or using the metro, but I'm not complaining. I've only ridden in a car twice in my life and I would be perfectly capable of continuing my life forever without doing it again. Too fast for something controlled by a human.

"I'm not sure . . ." Cora whispers to Grey, now having moved to the front of the group to hold hands with him. I could only hear the last part of the conversation but I can rightfully assume they're speaking about E. Lara steps in time with Tyl, wiping off her pristine white skirt every time excess leaves float her way.

From afar, we might even resemble a functional group of friends.

"What is this?" A strong voice resounds in my ear. I turn, stopping in front of a small office supplies shop.

E drops a Tirn into my hand.

"Is this yours? Why-"

"I *took* it."

"From where?"

He tilts his head towards the shop.

"You stole it?"

"I took it."

"You need to give it back."

"It seemed important."

"It is, that's why you need to give it back."

"Why is it so important?"

I stare at him, incredulous, "Why is a Tirn important?"

He stares back, forcing me to drop my gaze.

"Yes, why is it important?"

Confusion wracks my brain as I attempt to discern whether he's kidding or not. How could he not know? Even if he's not from Raleigh, Tirns are everywhere. *Everywhere.*

The anger inside me begins to boil. Obviously, he knows what it is. Tirns have the potential to be life or death in some ways, especially when it comes to protecting yourself. A burning laser, some people call it, a weapon and a tool. Hot enough to be a weapon, advanced enough to change, start, or even end a line of coding. In a society such as the one we live in, having that ability is incredibly important.

So important, in fact, that losing one would start the arduously long process of obtaining another one. With this in mind, the anger begins to bubble over quicker and quicker. My mind is overheating, thinking of all the possibilities that could happen after E's bullshit decision. Medicine that needs opening? Vehicle unlocking? House locking? None of it. It's not as if E could use it anyways, unless he has a copy of the owner's fingerprint.

Cora never should have moved to the front of the group. The second he has no supervision, something like this happens.

And he has dragged me right in the middle.

Kleptomaniac.

"Where did you find it?" I try to keep my voice calm. Anger isn't an emotion I'm used to.

The grey chains on E's jacket jostle in the wind, "Tell me what it is."

"For the love of God."

The second that E's face twists into an amused glare, I snap. I don't think there's anything that I hate more in this world than someone hurting another person solely because they refused to think about the consequences of their actions.

Blissful ignorance.

Closing my hand around the small cylindrical device, I storm through the doors of the shop in hopes of finding whoever owns it. Usually, I would despise confrontation like this but obviously E knows just how to make me forget my personality.

Luckily enough for me, the shop is far from crowded. It almost feels odd. Rows and rows of digital pencils, pens, binders, but yet only about three customers browse. Two of which are an older couple arm in arm as they stroll through the isles. If I had lost my Tirn, I would be searching high and low in the isles, attempting to retrace my steps. From what I've heard, people used to react the same way when they lost their phones, considering that it held tons of personal information, if I remember correctly.

Back when phones existed.

As I continue to walk, I try to find anyone who looks concerned, angry, what have you—

"Excuse me, sorry, is that yours?"

Thank god.

"I was actually trying to find whose it was," I mumble, catching E entering the shop through my peripheral, "I, um, found it on one of the shelves. I assumed someone accidentally sat it down."

A young red-headed woman laughs, failing to notice E as he leans against the door frame, "I must have. Thank you, darling, you're a miracle."

I plaster on a smile as best I can.

I'm going to kill him.

Maybe E will be the murdered one by the end of this.

The woman gratefully takes her Tirn, pressing the small silver button so that the beam comes to life and aims it towards her purse. A small click responds.

"I really do appreciate it," she nods quickly before hurrying out. It doesn't take long for me to do the same, walking as fast as possible.

"You're a miracle, *darling*, a miracle."

Against my deepest wishes, E has already caught up to me.

"You can't mock someone you just stole from," I whisper under my breath so only he could hear; the way he said *darling* sent an icy chill down my spine. The rest of the group must have gotten distracted as well, only a couple stores away from us.

"I didn't know it was hers."

"I don't think you would have cared."

My own venom surprises me.

"It was on the ground."

"Sure it was, that's why you handed it to me." Definitely not so that I would be the one accused if the woman saw us outside.

"You covered for me."

I stop, cracking my knuckles against my hip, "If you hadn't noticed, we're trying to get somewhere. I would very much not like to have the whole group wait for you to explain to the Thieves Defend why in the hell you would steal someone's Tirn."

"That's a stupid name."

I roll my eyes; I couldn't care less about his opinions.

"Thieves Defend, sounds like a fucking medieval—"

"I really hope whatever information you claim to have is actually useful so that there's a legitimate reason for all of us having to put up with you."

E smiles, a full, legitimate smile.

Suddenly, A hand reaches out to touch my arm, causing my heart to skitter. I hadn't realized just how bad my head was pounding.

Thankfully, I turn to find Grey.

"Let's go," Grey takes my hand. He must have walked up without my knowledge.

Shit.

Inevitably, I had to explain everything to Grey.

"I've never seen you that angry before."

Me either.

"I hate him," I scoff, "I really do."

"Welcome to the club. I don't know how Cora dealt with him as children."

That's likely one of the reasons they haven't seen each other in so long. If I was in Cora's position, I would have tried to forget about E too.

But . . .

"Maybe he wasn't as bad back then."

There's a small part of me that hopes he has a good reason behind the way he acts. I don't particularly enjoy hating people, especially if I don't know their whole history. However, E makes it close to impossible not to.

I glance at Grey, hoping to convey my sympathy. He has to be taking this hard.

"Cora won't tell me what happened between them," he reads my mind.

I nod.

"I guess it's not the right time."

Grey sighs, pulling his hair into a ponytail at the nape of his neck. He's wearing a thin blue mesh-jacket today, allowing the body glitter beneath to shine through. But, even despite all of the shimmer, he's not himself. He wants to know Cora's history so that he may help them, but he knows he has to be patient.

He has to wait.

"If it's as bad as it seems, it might never be the right time."

"Here."

The group freezes, searching around for any reason as to why we've stopped. There are no apartments or houses in sight, at least none that seem to be the center of Tyl's attention.

"Please do not tell me that I suffered through this expedition only to be met with some sort of hidden building; I've experienced one too many today."

At this point, we've all made a collective decision to ignore any of E's comments, so far it has done nothing but urge him on.

I miss when he was quiet.

E continues to ramble about Tyl's made-up living conditions as we walk into a narrow alley. The heat has been increasing ever since we arrived at the city and seems to have a love for this specific back way.

Rubbing a tired hand over my face, I internally make a mental note to avoid pants next time. Bad move on a hot day. I don't understand how Grey does it, wear a jacket all day, every day. Beads of sweat roll down my shoulder blades as Tyl takes a sharp turn in front of a large black ironed gate. Without warning, the gate swings open.

"Fucking—damn," Grey jumps back.

Tyl drops his Tirn back in his pocket, shooting an apologetic smile at Grey.

How could anyone be mad at that smile?

How could anyone be mad at him at all?

After everyone makes their way through the gate, Tyl closes it back, leaving next to no space at all as we file into an even smaller alley. I try to flatten myself against the bricks as best I can without knocking Lara over.

"Mama said no friends!" A voice appears near the dimly lit doorway, now opened slightly. A child's voice.

Tyl exhales as he moves towards the front, "Mama said you couldn't have any friends over, Lynia, not me."

"How many?" the young voice answers.

"Five, but one of them is Cora."

Who is now smiling.

The door swings open almost immediately, "Co Woah!"

I think Tyl is multiplying.

I don't believe I've ever seen two people resemble each other as much as Tyl and presumably his younger sister.

It's amazing.

As Cora lifts the running child into their arms, I catch a small glimpse of that same mesmerizing smile.

Obviously, Lynia enjoys Cora's company.

I think we all do.

Maybe except for E, of course.

Speaking of which, Cora tilts towards their brother, facing Lynia away.

E looks the embodiment of emotions. Lips pursed, eyes glazed, hands clasped behind his back.

"Everyone, this is my sister Lynia. Lynia, this is Meira, Grey, Lara . . . and E."

She takes a moment to analyze each of us as Tyl points. When he points to E, Lynia wriggles out of Cora's grasp and makes her way over to him. Her small, bare feet avoid rogue pine straw as well as our shoes, box braids stopping an inch above her shoulders.

She's wearing a long green dress, embroidered with silver trails of ivy. Like the embodiment of summer.

"You look mean," Lynia says flatly and Lara stifles a laugh with the back of her hand.

E inhales sharply, kneeling to Lynia's height.

We all hold our breath as we pray he has some clue how to treat children. This could go one of two ways, he's either an asshole and none of us are shocked, or he decides to remain neutral, likely with a side of annoyance.

"As many say, I suppose. But perhaps you'll change your mind," E takes something out of his pocket, sitting it gently in her hand and closing her small fingers around it, "Don't tell your brother."

Lynia runs two pinched fingers across her lips, mimicking a zipper, "I take it back."

"Appreciated."

Before running back into the house, she shows Cora her new treasure. A small piece of candy.

Well, I guess there was a third option.

You have to be joking.

How come he treats every human like they don't deserve to live but knows exactly how to win over a child?

Does he just constantly have candy in his pocket?

Is he actually, potentially a normal person?

My stomach drops as I realize that my theory might have been correct, that maybe he actually does have a reason for treating all of us like shit. Well, perhaps not a reason, but some sort of excuse. Some sort of origin.

Because, obviously, he has the capability of being a decent human being.

E clears his throat, likely trying to cover up his actions, "Don't look at me like that. We had to make sure she let us in, didn't we?"

I still don't buy it.

He was smiling while speaking to Lynia.

A true, genuine smile.

Laugh lines that changed from mysterious to almost lovely. There was something behind his eyes, similar to when the feeling of nostalgia makes your chest light, your worries almost disappear.

Perhaps he was remembering another time in his past. A past in which he didn't have to hide his true feelings with thorns and poison. With hatred and pain.

Maybe.

Only maybe.

'Maybe' appears to be a key word with him.

Tyl appears to be having the same epiphany. He searches E's face for any sort of crack below the surface, Cora's eyes reflecting the same motion.

"Who are you?" Cora asks.

I swallow. The softness of Cora's voice takes an immediate effect on the group. Grey completely stills as he places a weary hand on their back.

Despite E's lack of response, Cora continues, "You need to choose. Are you 'E' or are you my brother, the one who used to bike two miles every fucking day so that we could walk home together? Are you 'E' or are you the one who would stay up all night looking at the road out of your stupid ass window just for a glimpse of someone who didn't even love—?"

And just like that, it's as if the two siblings simply forgot about the four other pairs of eyes watching intently, including my own.

"*You!* You were the one who took that away from me. You had no fucking plan, did you? You thought everything was going to work out perfectly? For God fucking sake, Cora, it didn't. You want to know what happened afterwards? Guess. I want you to think real fucking hard and guess what happened afterward."

"How was I supposed to know? I thought they killed you! I thought they killed *both* of you!"

E's eyes grow wild as heat creeps up his neck, "They *did* kill you!"

"Nearly, no thanks to you!" Cora scoffs.

"You didn't tell me what you were planning!"

"I wasn't the only one who planned it," they take a step away from E, "and no, we didn't tell you because you refused to admit the situation we were in. What were we supposed to do?"

E licks his bottom lip, a futile attempt to calm himself down.

"She's gone, Cora, because of *both* of us. Mourn who I used to be for as long as you want, he died alongside her."

In the future, when I'm one day able to look back on this moment with a clear mind, maybe I'll eventually understand what the actual *fuck* is going on.

Someone they knew, someone that both E and Cora cared about, died?

Because of them?

Each sibling thought the other was dead?

Cora almost *did* die?

But, something they said while they were arguing did catch my attention. Something that brought my thoughts back to a distant dream:

"Get out."

"I'm not dealing with this again . . . I can't lose you for weeks like last time."

I only hear my thoughts. My thoughts tell me that I can't look at her, that she's dead to me. I run my fingers through my hair frantically as I clench my fists. Her voice is like a soft echo in my ear.

However, this time, it didn't feel like a dream. It felt like someone whispering into my ear, telling me a story. Telling me about a dream they had, not one that I experienced. It felt so foreign yet so real that it forced my eyes frantically closed.

They still remain closed at the moment, my palms applying as much pressure as possible to the sockets. Tyl clears his throat, "I, um, I think we should go inside."

That was the first time I've heard him stutter; the confidence slowly ebbing away at every syllable.

"Let's," E responds, tucking his hair behind his ears before practically beelining it through the open door.

Reluctantly, we all follow E inside, Tyl closing the door behind us. I realize too late that I'm entering a house that I've never been in before, which brings a whole new level of worry. I've always hated things like this. Breaking something that doesn't belong to me, suddenly becoming lost, getting caught in an unpleasant conversation, and so on, are all irrational fears that have a firm grasp on my mind whenever I enter into someone's home.

My parents' coworkers happen to be the creators of these fears. Not only are they extremely awkward, but they also treat me like a child. Saying that someone my age cannot possibly be correct; that they'll only believe me once my parents confirm it. They find it amusing to make comments like "Every time I see you, I still picture you as *this big!*" or "You used to be a lot friendlier, huh?" I'm not exactly sure how my shyness came across as unfriendliness, as they're the only ones that have ever said that. I guess I can only hope it's not true.

It's not.

But what if it is?

It's not.

Luckily, however, based on the personalities of Tyl and Lynia, I can trust that any other family members will be extraordinarily kind. This thought, mixed with the need to form some sort of idea with the group about what to do, are the only reasons I have to remain calm. Getting locked into my mind is not an option at the moment, especially considering the walls of my brain feel like they're caving in. After remembering that dream, I don't think what I'm experiencing could even be described as a headache anymore. An implosion, perhaps, but definitely not just a headache.

The only relief I see fit would be taking the time to admire the world that I just strolled into.

I say *world* because I feel like I've stepped into another dimension. Tyl's home is ornately decorated, covered with an expanse of colors that could be considered dramatic, if not for the interior design. I can say without a doubt that whoever decorated this room is a professional. There's a sense of calmness and connection that never drips over into crowdedness.

Tulle hangs from the high ceilings and spreads to each of the space's four corners, connecting with the lavender curtains. Lynia lounges on the circular couch surrounding a small fireplace as she watches our reactions. I could never imagine living in this home, waking up every morning to *this*. Lynia stares at me, pride prickling the corners of her mouth, "Just wait until you see Tyl's room."

I smile back, warmth radiating through my entire body. I never thought that design could have such an effect on me but yet I'm standing here suddenly, in a foreign place, with barely a worry. On the contrary, besides the pain that I'm attempting to ignore, I feel extremely comfortable. Comfortable enough to only feel a slight tinge of annoyance as E chimes in with another senseless comment.

"I actually would much prefer to not go into his bedroom, is there any other place we could all speak? An office, or such?"

Figures.

"You chose to come with us," Cora lowers their voice. "Don't act as if you're forced to be here."

E shrugs, the whites of his teeth appearing slightly through his small grin.

Apart from his personality, he would most likely be considered attractive.

If it didn't physically hurt me to look at him then perhaps, I would admire his features more than I do, but my annoyance towards him takes precedence. Precedence over admiration. Maybe one day I'll be able to look at him without him taking notice, not in a creepy way, but just so that he doesn't have any excuse to grow his ego to new heights. I fully believe that if that happens it would be the death of him by the hands of every single one of us.

"Do you want to share *your* information or not? If so, we're doing it in my room."

E brings himself closer, standing mere inches away from Tyl, but he doesn't budge.

"Do you want to share your information or not? You said that you had something for us, didn't you?"

Tyl begins to study E, "It's a physical object, not information, and I don't think I remember including you when I brought that up."

Wow.

Tyl has lost patience.

If we were to ignore the real people present in this debate, then it could almost be mistaken as flirting.

"It's a conspiracy, isn't it? You seem like the type."

"Why would I bring everyone here in order to just talk about a conspiracy?" Tyl crosses his arms against the white of his sweater.

"See, that's exactly what every conspiracist says but yet somehow they always seem to make up a reason to spew something unreasonable."

Suddenly, Lynia makes a hard scoff which catches E off guard, and breaks him from his game.

"I bet you can't even spell the word conspiracist. You know, Petrichor might not allow kids my age to enter the library, but they did teach me how to read."

And, just like that, I love her already.

E seems to falter as his mouth opens and closes again, snapping his gaze towards Cora. I can see them swallow with force while their brother looks almost as if he just witnessed a betrayal. It wasn't fear, though, but disappointment and reluctance; reluctance to accept. To accept *what*, I have no idea. I doubt that it was Lynia's hostility that caused the reaction, which means that it was something within her words.

"Lynia, could you get the book for us?"

She studies her brother with distaste, "Mom's in her office, I can't."

A sudden fear rockets through my brain.

Are we not supposed to be here?

Tyl said it was fine, but maybe he was just being hospitable.

"Tyl, if we shouldn't be here—"

He cuts me off gently, "It's okay, I promise."

Somehow, this does absolutely nothing to reassure me.

"Tell your mother that we're here," Cora whispers. "When she comes up, Lynia can grab the book."

For the first time, I finally realize just how close Cora and Tyl are. Lynia is obviously extremely comfortable around them, and Cora seems to know their mother as well, not to mention whatever this book is.

"You okay with that, Lyn?" Cora sits down next to her.

"Mhmm, I'll go get her."

Tyl and I chuckle lightly as Lynia scampers off.

His laughter is as contagious as his smile, perfectly sculpted.

That's exactly how I would describe Tyl: perfectly sculpted in every way shape and form.

He spills a joke about how his sister only ever listens to Cora, and I can't help but match his gaze. "She said she'll be up in a couple of minutes," Lynia states, quickly taking her seat next to Cora once again.

"We can talk in my room in the meantime," Tyl turns towards E. "Feel free to stay in here and chat with Lynia, if you would rather . . ."

Based on E's silence I can tell that he still hasn't recovered from whatever had thrown his personality off balance; or perhaps he does really want to speak to Tyl's sister.

Whatever the reason is, no one seems to disagree as we all follow Tyl down a narrow hallway. Some part of my mind forces my head to swivel back to E despite my reluctance.

He looks almost morbid.

Unfathomably miserable, maybe, the exact opposite of the person in the forest.

Before that tinge of guilt can grow any larger in the pit of my stomach, E slowly raises his middle finger, head tilted down to hide his silent grin.

"Jesus Christ," I whisper and turn back around.

You know, sometimes I feel proud about how I decorated my

room; don't get me wrong, I still am, but I can never compare to the one that I just stepped into. My eyes first shoot to the ceiling where a circular gray light creates a sort of bubble, green vines twirling around its base. These vines then continue across the ceiling and down the cream-colored walls to pool gracefully onto the floor. Tyl's bed sits across from the door, beautifully made, a mix of dark green and gray geometric shapes scattering the blankets. Even though the only other contents of the room are a neat desk and a grey dresser, the vines do more than enough to make the room full, cozy. Comfortable.

"This can't be real."

Concluding all of our thoughts perfectly, it was Lara who spoke up this time. Tyl stands with his hands loosely behind his back as Grey runs a vine through his fingers.

"Fully real."

I don't even know what to say. My mouth continues to open and close but nothing comes to mind. *How am I supposed to respond to this?* I didn't even notice the plush rug underneath my feet, making me want nothing more than to sink to the floor and sleep.

"I, um . . . I had help," Tyl laughs breathlessly.

Cora sits crisscross on his bed and closes their eyes, Grey leaning his head on their shoulder. I'm glad that they have Grey as a comfort.

He's amazing at it.

I know that he has to be feeling extremely confused, maybe even hurt, but he tries hard not to show it for Cora's sake.

Lara slumps onto the floor and pulls me down with her, letting me finally relax by shifting against her.

"Can I ask what the book is?"

Tyl remains standing, "It's a notebook that my mom found

years ago, so she says, no names on it or anything like that. It holds information about some type of liquid, again no name for it, but it was obviously important for someone to have written so many pages about it. Cora and I have both read every single word, and we agreed that the liquid was described as extremely useful. Useful enough to start a new government. Useful enough, perhaps, to start Petrichor. But, the reason why I wanted to show it to all of you, was because it reminded me of how you described the smoke outside of the shed. The liquid, whatever it is, can be put into a gaseous state."

We all stare at him.

"How," I pause, searching for words, "how do you know Petrichor is involved with this notebook?"

"Well, the logo on the front cover helped," Cora explains.

How a *liquid* could help to form a whole new government, I can't even imagine.

But, at the same time, it seems as if my dreams can.

I knelt down and reached out my hand as the dog lightly placed it down. Its whole body wriggled, waiting. I looked closer into the vial. Brown bubbling liquid, almost like soda, swirled around continuously.

No, no.

No.

I'm not psychic. There is a remote chance that the liquid in my dream is the same as the notebook.

I take that back.

There is no chance.

This is not some type of foreshadowing bullshit.

"For fuck's sake, Sydney Carton, you can come in, you know."

I bite the inside of my cheek, searching for any recognition of the person Cora just mentioned. Who the hell is Sydney Carton? No idea.

E remains transfixed to the doorway and ignores Cora's comment. I think this is the longest he's ever gone without speaking.

Unfortunately, as if he heard my thoughts, he breaks that record.

"Lynia wants to talk to you."

"Tell her that she can come in here," Tyl starts.

"No, not you," E points to me, "she wants her."

"Oh."

That's all I can manage.

Why would she want me?

Nobody seems to have any objections, so I steady myself and rise to stand, waiting for E to continue.

"She's still in the living room."

I partly thought that he was going to follow me back to Lynia, but I relax as he holds his stance where he is.

Before I can reach the living room, however, I am met with only darkness.

Chapter Fifteen

April 1, 2073
9:00 AM

S hit

That hurts.

Not a normal hurt, not the type of hurt that I'm used to, but a hurt like no other. I hurt everywhere. Everywhere. Inside and out.

I know it's morning.

I can hear the birds outside my window, but they sound fake, muffled as if they're underwater. As I shuffle around my blankets in an attempt to get up, I can tell that the rest of the world sounds like that too.

What did I do last night? Yesterday? My head throbs even trying to remember.

Drugs? I don't think so. I mean, I don't even know how I would get those, much less be in the right mindset to enjoy them.

I need to open my eyes.

Fuck.

Work.

Shit, I have to go to work, which means I have to open my eyes.

Okay.

One.

Two.

Three.

I do it.

And it is a mistake.

Sunlight shocks my vision as the room swirls around me.

Now I feel like *I'm* underwater.

How can I be underwater and in a full sweat at the same time?

It's slowing though, which is good; my hearing seems to be returning to normal as well.

Maybe this isn't so bad. Maybe this wouldn't be so bad if my arm didn't feel like it was being bit by a snake every other second.

Lifting up my sleeve carefully, I try to avoid angering the serpent.

It doesn't work.

Pain bursts through every damn nerve I have, making colors dull around me. The room spins, but I'm able to lock my gaze on my arm. What isn't dull, however, would be the purple of the bruise mixing with the dried blood plastered to my skin.

What the *fuck* happened last night?

Even though I know I should be feeling a large surge of panic, I feel nothing. Nothing.

If my parents were here right now, maybe I wouldn't be so calm. Maybe them freaking out would make me freak out.

But they're not here, and I'm not freaking out.

However, their business trips never last this long, so perhaps I should be.

I manage, despite the pain, to ready myself and leave the house with minimal delay. I have hidden my wound with a long sleeve shirt. a surprising action given my current state of mind. My mind still swirls trying to remember how I hurt myself, where I was, what happened, but I can't. It's like I'm pounding against a concrete wall blocking me from memories that were somehow taken from me. Somehow lost. Every time the concrete cracks, I'm set into a fit of shattering pain.

But, in any case, I'm still trudging along carefully towards the library. Somehow.

I hope Izmene won't be able to notice the color under my eyes or the lack of thoughts in my mind.

"You walk at a snail's pace do you know that?"

I whirl around, trying to locate the source of the voice even though I know exactly who it is.

E is standing a few feet away, hands in his pockets. He's wearing a white button down with a black blazer overtop, his hair resting in a ponytail at the nape of his neck. And glasses, he's wearing glasses.

I sigh, continuing to walk, "you continue to exhibit stalker tendencies."

"Do you think you would be the one I would stalk?"

He matches his step with mine.

"Seems to be that way."

E shakes his head, "you would be the last on my list."

I wait for him to say why, to say that I'm not interesting or whatever other insult he can come up with, but he doesn't.

"Are those real?"

E doesn't even glance my way as he taps the lens of his glasses, "You tell me."

"I didn't think you would ever admit to having any type of defect."

Physical, especially.

This makes him turn towards me, "Not a defect, angel, but a

tool. See, with one simple gesture," E removes the frames from his face, waving a hand towards me, "Whatever is plaguing me in my general vicinity immediately disappears."

Funny.

Especially because he's the one that started this conversation in the first place. I would have been perfectly fine without having to deal with him today.

"Can I ask you a question?"

"Desirably not about my vision, or lack thereof."

"Why are you following me?"

He considers for a moment, looking at me with a gaze I can't read.

"If I answer, you have to answer a question of my own."

"Fine."

"I had to go to the library today to grab records, and I saw you walking the same way. So, in other words, I'm not following you, but it seems that they are."

He tilts his head back slightly, signaling to something behind him. As nonchalant as possible, I turn to look at what he's talking about, *if* he's actually telling the truth and people are following me.

Two Petrichor workers are indeed there, walking the same way as us, looking at us.

'They've been there since you left your house."

Well shit.

"Why would . . . does that mean you've been walking behind me the whole time?"

E grins, not allowing a full smile, "yes, but it took me a bit to catch up to you."

"I thought you said I was walking at a snail's pace?"

"I never said that I wasn't either."

Annoying.

"Well maybe they're doing the same thing that you are."

"And what would that be?"

"Not being stalkers," I run a hand through my hair.

"Perhaps."

Why would Petrichor workers be following me? I mean I know that we might have seen something we shouldn't when it comes to the shed, and I have connections to Ignite, but why follow me specifically? Why not anyone else in our group?

Unless it has something to do with my parents, but again, why follow me? Why not just come up to me and ask whatever they need to know or tell me whatever they need to?

"You said you would answer a question of mine."

I really would rather not.

"Go ahead."

"Who did you lose a fight with?"

What?

I turn towards him, searching his face for any hint of what he means. Amusement plasters his features as he points towards his eyes.

Ah. He's talking about the color.

"I didn't get punched, if that's what you're asking. I just haven't slept well."

E stays silent for a moment, our footsteps the only sound.

"Why?"

Why haven't I slept well? I could give him a thousand and one reasons.

"There's a lot going on."

All he does is nod.

No insult, no quip, nothing.

"My turn. Why haven't you or Izmene mentioned the fact that you're—"

He interrupts, "family? Unless you would like to hear my whole life history, I don't think I can answer that question."

If it would give me some answers, I honestly wouldn't mind it.

"Fine, I'll let that one pass. Where did you get the knife?"

Without hesitation, he moves his blazer and grabs the hilt from his waist line. It immediately lights up green.

"Cora and I were each given one as children. They were specifically made for only us to use, hence the green."

My stomach drops a bit. I have a way in, a way to ask a multitude of different questions. But should I push it? Should I push him?

Might as well try, just a bit.

"Given by your parents?"

He stops, forcing us both to cease walking, forcing me to match his eye contact.

"So now we're allowed to ask personal questions?"

There's no anger in his voice, just pure curiosity. If this leads somewhere, maybe I can get other answers. What happened between him and Cora, what he does with the records, so on and so forth. Honestly, I could probably come up with questions for days.

"Sure," I shrug, "Why not."

At this point, I think I would much rather have answers than be saved from having to respond to whatever question he may ask.

He takes a step forward again, walking now with a much slower speed, "Yes, our parents gave them to us. They thought they would be useful for whatever twisted reasons they could come up with."

I nod, having to look away from the expression on his face. Malice, pain, anger.

Perhaps I shouldn't have pushed.

"What is your reason for joining Ignite?"

It takes me a moment to register what he asked.

"That's your personal question?"

I don't know what I was expecting, but it definitely was not that. I thought he would ask something insulting, or maybe something that I wouldn't want to answer, anything like that.

"Indeed. Answer."

"I . . . I guess that I don't like the feeling of not doing anything. I learn about girls from the old world that have already accomplished incredible things by the time they were my age and . . . I don't know. I feel like in order to accomplish anything, I have to understand the world that I'm living in, and I think Ignite can help with that."

The answer spills out of my mouth before I can even think. I guess it's been in the back of my brain for a while now, the reason for all of this, the origin of the curiosity towards Petrichor.

"Ignite, or Tyl?"

I stare at him, the only thought in my mind being the fact that I'm grateful we're almost at the library.

"Were you really only asking that question to see what I would say about Tyl?"

E shrugs, "perhaps."

"I was asking you real questions while you just wanted to figure out how you could insult him next? To see if I would play into whatever sick fantasy you have of Tyl and I in your head."

"So now you believe I have fantasies about you?"

He makes me want to scream.

"You think that we're together, or want to be, and you want me to admit it."

"You can only admit something that's true."

I roll my eyes as we finally reach the library, "You're difficult, do you understand that? So fucking difficult."

E smiles then, seemingly surprised by my tone.

"I can be a multitude of different things."

When he sees that I'm heading for the front door, he only lets out a sigh of amusement before heading towards the back of the building.

⁂

As the door closes behind me, I feel like I can barely breathe.

"This isn't like you." Its Izmene.

Not even one foot in the door and I'm already found out.

"What?" I ask, eyes tiredly swiveling toward Izmene.

"Late."

Luckily, for the state of my employment, Izmene is smiling. She wears a white pantsuit this time, her hair worn very similar to Cora's.

"I'm sorry, I—"

"I understand, Meira. No explanation needed."

I nod, trying to push down this lingering small amount of concern swirling around my head.

Maybe nothing is wrong with me and everything is perfectly normal; just a bad night's rest.

Maybe.

As I begin to go through records and chat lightly with Izmene, that's what I have to believe. Normality. Normality is key. If I focus on normal then I won't focus on my arm, my mind, my feelings.

"How is E?" she asks.

I almost drop an album.

So much for normality.

She knows, then. She knows I've met E, that we've all met E.

"He's- he's . . . I don't really know. Him and Cora don't seem to get along."

A small part of me hopes she'll offer some insight into their relationship, some type of answer for something that really isn't even any of my business.

Izmene takes a long breath, stopping in her work to evaluate the bracelet on her wrist, "They're young, and they've been through so much. More than I could handle at any age. They were bound to disagree at some point."

Closer.

"What did they used to be like?"

I know that they had to have been friendly to each other at one point, purely based on the pain in both of their voices when they scream at each other.

"Cora is much the same, which is a good thing. They have always been determined and are a huge help to me when I need it. E, on the other hand, is nothing like how he used to be. He lost himself at some point or another and can't seem to get that back. Though, sometimes, I can still see little specks of his old self which help me hold out hope. They're very similar in ways that they can't see themselves. I've tried to tell them, both of them, but they'll hear none of it," Izmene laughs a bit at the last part, like a grandmother telling a joke about her stubborn grandchildren.

Which, though it's still hard for me to believe, is the truth.

One grandchild, in particular, is much more than stubborn. He used to be different, but no one can tell me what changed. Maybe they don't know, or maybe they don't want to tell. I know he doesn't, that's for sure. It seems as if the only thing E wants to do is complete whatever goal he has in mind, whatever endgame he's playing. I can see it in his eyes, that motivation, and though perhaps it should scare me, it does the opposite.

I want to know what it is. What he wants. What he's doing.

But, one thing I do know, he refuses to change, and seemingly so does Cora.

Has it been a week since I met them both? A month? I can't really tell anymore. Time has been going by slowly recently. Or perhaps, too fast.

"How did you manage that?"

I startle, realizing late that my sleeve had slid down to reveal my wound as I reached for a top shelf.

Too quickly, I attempt a response, "I'm not sure."

Izmene doesn't seem to buy it. Taking a step closer to me, she carefully rolls up my sleeve until the entire wound is revealed. I hold my breath.

"There's a darker spot in the middle, is that what hurts the most?"

I nod.

"Tell me," she swallows, "if it gets any worse."

I nod again, slower this time.

She has some sort of gleam in her eye, and I can't determine what it is. All I know is that she's suspicious of something, whether that something be me or the cause of the dark colors painting my arm, I'm not sure.

"You asked about them, and I know that you're getting closer to Cora, so maybe you'll like this."

Izmene takes out her wallet, leather and tattered.

I like it. It reminds me of the old world.

"Here."

I realize that I'm looking at a picture of E and Cora as children, but I can't fully comprehend it.

E is smiling.

Not a mysterious, false grin but a real genuine smile. Cora is doing the same as they hold hands with their brother. They're both wearing thick jackets, holding old winter hats in their small hands. E has the same dark brown curls and brown eyes, still completely contrasting with Cora and their blonde hair.

"Who's this?" I ask, pointing to the third figure standing next to Cora, the only one not smiling.

"An old friend of Cora's, his name was Ezra. He was a nice kid but he got wrapped up with the wrong group as he got older. Your friend, Lara, I believe he's her brother."

Ezra.

Ezra and Cora used to be friends?

The only comments I've heard about Ezra were from Lara and sometimes her parents, none of which were positive. He abandoned them.

Has Lara been connected to E and Cora somehow, and didn't even realize it? Has she not mentioned their names to her parents, or do they just not remember their son's childhood friends?

Perhaps they wanted to forget.

The more confusing aspect, however, would be why both Cora and E didn't seem to know who Lara was when they first met her, or at least if they did, they were extremely good at hiding it.

"Is that why he moved to Korea, to get away from the wrong crowd?"

Izmene looks at me for a moment, confusion dancing across her features.

"Yes . . . Korea. I guess it is."

My head rests in my hands, defeated.

I haven't left the library yet even though I finished up about an hour ago.

Izmene still gave me a twenty, despite my lateness, which caused a tinge of guilt in my stomach. Grey won't be happy about that. I don't even know how much they've been getting paid. Hell, I don't even know what they've been doing at work.

I haven't asked

Haven't had the time

Haven't had the focus.

I stuff the small currency into my pocket and wait on the front steps for Lara and Grey. Maybe I should ask them. Should be a good friend.

"Oh, thank god, Ira! You scared the shit out of us."

Grey barrels into me, cradling my head against his chest like a small child. I hear Lara sit down next to me.

"Scared you?"

How could I have scared them?

Unless it has something to do with yesterday, which I still can't quite place.

"Check your damn Tirn, you didn't answer the night we all left Tyl's house or yesterday."

My head starts to throb as I reluctantly take out the cylindrical device. Clicking the small blue button on the top, the screen materializes. Six missed calls, twenty-three unopened messages. Shit. I remember going to Tyl's house but after that . . . nothing.

I try to appear nonchalant, "What happened at Tyl's house?"

Grey suddenly releases me, blue eyes piercing my own.

"Nope, not happening. I'm not gonna let you act all innocent as if you didn't look at E like you had fucking fallen in love with him or something."

My stomach drops as something in my chest begins to scream with pain.

I.

Did.

What?

I feel the blood rush from my face. I stare down at the stone steps, eyes wide, unfocused in the shock.

"And then," Grey continues, "after reading more through that notebook and E explaining that he 'thinks' the shed is owned by Petrichor, Tyl decided that we should leave some things, like the book and the shed, untouched. He said that they were too dangerous. He didn't want anyone getting hurt. I could tell that you weren't particularly fond of that idea, but you didn't say anything. Honestly, that isn't even the most important part, I'm still mulling over the fact that you looked at E like—"

"Grey, stop."

Notebook? What notebook?

I look between the two of them, some silent plea that they would say they were joking, that none of this happened. They don't, though, and so I'm now stuck with the fact that my memory of the last two days is entirely shot.

That the memory issues brought up in the Ignite meetings are very much true.

And I have now become a part of the problem.

"We didn't know where you were, who to call. We tried your parents, Tyl, hell even E, but of course he doesn't own a fucking Tirn for some reason. Nothing. Meira, what is going on?" Lara speaks softly, and I can hear the worry laced into her words.

With a broken mind, I answer, "My parents are on a business trip. I . . . I don't know what happened. I haven't spoken to Tyl," I swallow, "or E."

Lie, but they don't need to know about the walk here.

They continue to ask questions, so many questions, until they determine that I truly cannot remember anything after arriving at Tyl's house. The more questions, the more I feel reality slip out from under me. I feel like the sky is falling, pressing me flat again the cool concrete slabs of the steps, the trees pushing me down deeper.

How did I not even realize? How did I not think about Tyl's house or the fact that I was there and then suddenly in my bed? Nothing in between?

I didn't even question it. I just thought I was tired, stressed, what have you.

Shit.

Maybe I can relate to E losing himself, in one way or another.

"Alright, get up," Lara insists. "We're going to a doctor."

This wakes me up.

"No, no. No we're not."

"I agree with Lara. I mean, obviously this is happening to other people and is an actual fucking issue outside of yourself. We don't know what will happen if we let it continue."

Shut up, Grey.

"I'm fine, really. I just need more sleep," I try, not exactly sure whether I'm attempting to convince them or myself. Maybe both.

"You slept all day yesterday and obviously it didn't do shit."

I stare at them.

They say I slept, but I feel as if I've been hit by a bus.

"How did I get home, after Tyl's place?"

"You just . . . we all took the metro back. You walked home. Everything was normal, Meira."

Lara looks devastated.

Grey looks devastated.

I'm devastated.

I feel the tears slip down my cheeks before I even realize I'm crying.

I'm stuck.

My mind isn't my own anymore. All I can do is watch as all control is taken from me.

Until I'm nothing.

Grey's strong hands touch my face, wiping the tears away, "you're not alone. This is happening, everywhere, not just with the people connected to Ignite. We heard more about it yesterday, I think Petrichor is trying to keep it under wraps. You're not alone, but you need to see a doctor."

No.

No, I can't.

I can't lose control like that, admit that something's wrong.

I can't.

It will go away, whatever this is, it has to.

If Petrichor is trying to keep this under wraps, will the doctors even be willing to help? Will they turn me in, force me into secrecy?

That's a stretch, I know, but after everything that E explained I can't keep the theories out of my head.

If Petrichor was really willing to help, they would say something about it. They would . . . I don't know, comfort people. The fact that Grey and Lara heard more about it shows that Petrichor has to know about it by now, heard that it's happening to a multitude of different people.

But yet, nothing. Nothing has been said, that any of us know of.

I can't do this.

I can't do this right now.

I need to change the subject.

What happened before I was talking to them? Something important. It was something important. What was it? Izmene showed me something. Something that had to do with Lara. The picture. It was the picture. Cora, E, and . . . who? Who was it?

Ezra.

"Did you know that E and Cora used to know your brother?"

Lara stares at me.

I probably shouldn't have said that, her brother is a tight subject.

However, I needed to tell her, I needed her to know.

"What? Meira, this has nothing to do with—"

I wrack my brain for the right words.

This is hard for both of them, I'm not oblivious to that, as it not only brings up Ezra but also gives Grey another secret that Cora has kept from him. I would have done it at a different time if I could have, but the subject change was extremely necessary.

Especially considering the fact that I might have forgotten about it in a couple of days, in my current situation, if I had waited.

"Izmene showed me a picture," I clear my throat, "of them when they were younger. She said it was Ezra."

Lara runs a hand through her dark hair. "No, actually, I didn't know that. Did you?" she asks Grey, her tone a mix of anger and confusion.

He shakes his head.

"That's it, we're figuring this shit out," Grey stands. "I've been letting it slide so far in the hope that eventually Cora would tell me about their past but now that it involves Ezra, it raises the stakes. They're breaking inside, the longer they have to deal with E, the longer they don't talk to anyone about whatever it is that happened. I know I shouldn't look into something Cora told me not to, but I need to know how to help them. They're not gonna let me otherwise."

Lara nods, "and you're sure Meira, that it was him?"

"Yes."

I see where this is going, and I'm ready.

I'm excited.

Not only do I have the possibility of figuring out why I get that same odd feeling whenever I'm around this family, but I get to investigate E, as he doesn't seem too fond about sharing his past either. I get to understand him, why he acts like he does.

Especially with me.

"Cora might—"

"They'll be fine, they'll understand. We're doing this. However," he turns on me, "don't think this will make us forget about taking you to a doctor, Ira, that's still happening, trust me."

Cora will not understand. Grey knows that. And I know that if I give it a few days, they'll forget about the doctor.

Especially if I'm fine.

Which I will be.

"How are we doing this, exactly?" Lara asks.

"Well, let's go right to the source. Do you know when Izmene leaves, Ira?"

Perhaps.

Apparently, there's a different exit out of the library considering that I've been sitting on the front steps and I never saw Izmene leave, and we're fairly certain she's not here. Not only have we called her name, but we've checked almost all of the rooms as well. Almost all of them.

"Hey, you guys stay here. I'm going to check one more place," I state as I begin to walk away, not giving them the chance to refute despite their unwavering stares behind my back. I can tell that they don't want to let me out of their sight. That they're scared I'll disappear once more. Hell, maybe I will.

How would I know?

But, like I said, everything is fine.

Everything.

Except for the fact that I need to check one last place.

Technically, yes, we are about to go through Izmene's things for any hint of hidden history, but that doesn't mean I want to betray her trust fully by showing them the record room.

There's a line.

I might be the one who drew that line, but it's still there. Attempting to keep my footfalls as silent as possible, I make my way to the door and continuously check behind me at almost every step.

"Izmene?" I whisper. No answer. Even though the room could barely fit two queen beds inside, I insist on sweeping the room over multiple times before I feel a bit more satisfied.

Good.

"Oh, so this is *illegal* illegal. I mean, personally, I love it."

"Who would have thought, Grey, our Meira growing up to be just a teensy bit of a criminal?"

I freeze at the sound of their voices.

Not good.

At this point, what else could go wrong?

I've lost memories, presumably my mind, presumably my parents, and I'm quite close to losing all feeling in my arm.

Why not lose my job too?

"I'm sorry, didn't I tell you two to stay out there? Maybe I misheard my own voice?" The chill in my tone comes across as clearly as it was meant to, but the intended audience only chuckles lightly. They're not used to this, me acting like this, and neither am I.

I still enjoy it, nonetheless.

"No secrets allowed here, you know this," Lara smiles.

She begins to flip through the records as Grey occupies the only chair in the room, an old rolling office chair that is almost as unstable as my mind at the moment. He begins to spin in small circles,

"So, I have a question for you, Ira. Do you deny the fact that you're working in an illegal career field? I assume this is where you sneak off to for work, right?"

"It's not technically illegal," I sigh, "just also not technically Petrichor approved."

Grey's light eyebrows shoot up at that, reeling at my lack of denial.

"What's in it for you?" Lara asks.

Nothing.

But I can't exactly say that.

I can't really say that Izmene has this capacity to make me feel like I'm where I'm supposed to be.

Cora does too.

But not E.

And I swear he never will.

"I like music. I enjoy learning about how the world used to be. Put those together, and I'm here."

I mean, I'm not lying. But, even so, they don't buy it.

"Is that so? Because I was considering that you were doing this so that Izmene would give you her blessing to spend time with her . . . Grandson, perhaps?"

I pinch the bridge of my nose in frustration; it isn't even worth a response. I started working for Izmene before I even knew that E was related.

"You've spent time with him, haven't you? Please don't tell me that you guys have . . ."

"Grey!" Lara and I react at once, attempting to put his mental filter back in place.

"I hate him, Grey, you know that. I hate him just as much as the rest of us, why in the hell would I do anything with him? Also, I'm extremely confused as I seem to remember recently you trying to convince me to go after Tyl."

He only smiles, "Oh no, trust me, I am fully on Tyl's side. But I don't think you are."

I want this to stop.

I want no more questions, and I sure as hell don't want them knowing that E keeps popping up in places that he shouldn't be.

That he continues to question me just like I question him.

"I'm on no one's side, Grey. Tyl is a friend, and I think he considers me the same. E is E. There's nothing to say about him."

Just the possibility of thinking about E in that way almost makes me physically sick.

I think his personality would repulse anyone.

"There might not be anything to say about his personality, obviously, but his *looks*—"

"Just because he looks good doesn't make up for anything."

"So you agree on his looks?" Lara joins in, making me feel slightly betrayed.

I repeat once more, "It doesn't make up for anything. Where did this come from, Grey? Nothing's changed."

He shakes his head, jest beginning to turn into something close to concern, "everything's changed. You've changed, and I think you're the only one that hasn't noticed it. The way you've been speaking recently, the way you've been acting, it's all new, and not even to mention the memory stuff. Lara and I have been talking, and—"

I turn my gaze on Lara for confirmation, but she's staring at the floor. Et tu, brute?

"—we agreed that something changed. I'm not saying it's bad . . . but it's different."

I swallow.

Inhale.

Exhale.

"I don't know what you're talking about, I'm sorry."

But yet, I do.

I know that I've been acting differently. That something has grown inside of me that seems to be dictating my every move, my every word. I think it's ambition. Ambition to understand, ambition to not comply to something that I know nothing about, ambition to take control of my life. I've been caring less about what people think, and more about myself, more about what I want to accomplish.

And as of right now, I want to know the world around me. In a way, I don't think Lara and Grey will understand that. They might not trust Petrichor, but they enjoy life. I know that they do. However, I'm not sure if I ever have. I've felt out of place, wrong, for as long as I can remember. And I want that to change.

Eventually, after a moment of silence, they decide to yield, ignoring the fact that it was only so that they could move to a different hot topic. Personally, I never thought that they would care so much about the records, yet they seem infatuated with what got me into this situation, asking me questions I don't know the answers to. *How long has this been going on? I don't know. Is Izmene the only one who does this?* I don't know. *Who are Bird and Cliff?* I don't know, I only read the names off of a note like they did.

"Maybe her grandchildren?"

Exhausted, I whisper, "Maybe."

"I think we've gotten ourselves involved in some deep family shit."

I look at Lara with a sense of foreboding.

We really don't know anything about this family.

Anything

But yet our lives seem to continually intertwine with theirs.

"We're making a pact, my friends. Since we're all severely lacking in entertainment, besides Meira's memory loss of course," Grey states, enlightening me on the fact that maybe they aren't, thankfully, taking my issues increasingly seriously, "I believe that we should do everything we possibly can to learn about them. For my sake with Cora, for Ira's with her lover, and for Lara with her brother, now that apparently, he's back in the picture. But, considering that I just so happen to be incredibly in love with Cora, there should be some boundaries. Boundaries in which we won't define currently but also won't cross once we get to them."

I choose to ignore his choice of words. *Lover* is a word that should never be used in this context, with *him*, but quite frankly should also never be used in terms of me.

As of right now, at least.

"Let's." Lara nods.

"Alright, but not for the reason you said."

For many other reasons, but not for that one.

For every other reason.

Chapter Sixteen

April 22, 2073

6:15 AM

Sleep.

That would be nice, to be able to sleep again.

I can't, simply put.

Can't sleep. Can't eat.

Well, I take that back.

I can eat grapes.

I can only eat grapes. Anything else and I'm kneeling in front of the toilet while my stomach rebels against itself.

Grapes are good, though. Grapes are very good.

It's been like this for weeks. Three, to be exact.

What else has happened?

My parents are back. However, 'back' is a physical term, not a mental one. Yes, they are currently back in our house. No, they both are very much not here mentally. I've tried to talk to them. I've tried everything. "Work is hard, Meira," and "everything is fine, sweetheart, we promise," oh and my favorite "how have classes been going?" I've gotten that comment three times now. See, it would be an innocent question if I was indeed in classes and they were indeed wondering how they were. The problem is I'm not, and they should know that. My classes have been like this for years.

And yet they still asked.

Three times.

I'm blaming it on stress.

If I didn't, then I would be having much bigger issues.

Over the last weeks, I've seen Lara and Grey many times and each time they attempt once more to get me to remember what happened at Tyl's house. To get me to see a doctor.

It hasn't succeeded.

At this point, I've accepted it. I mean, it hasn't happened again so, why care?

If I did, then I would be having much bigger issues.

They haven't tried to speak to my parents about it, but even if they did, I'm not sure if my parents would even react.

I'm not even sure they would care.

Despite these fruitless attempts, we have all been sticking to our pact. Or at least trying. Izmene has become very quiet around me, so much so that I worry she found out about Grey and Lara and the record room. I know that she hasn't, but it still worries me.

Everything worries me. Especially right now.

But I wasn't about to break the pact.

I decided that if Izmene wouldn't talk to me, then the next subject that wasn't already being investigated would unfortunately be E. I decided this about two and a half weeks ago and since then, I have not seen E once. No one has. Not that anyone minds, especially me, but for knowledge's sake he couldn't have disappeared at a worse time. Because of this poor choice, I sadly haven't been able to help much. Neither has Lara. Whenever she tries to mention Ezra and his childhood to her parents, they shove her off. Ezra is too much of a fresh wound to them, and bringing up his childhood when he was still with them likely does not help the situation. So, she met a dead end. Lara even tried to look through photo albums and old trinkets and such, all to no avail. It almost seems like Ezra, or his parents, completely erased his existence. Which, as a matter of fact, really fucks up what we're trying to do here.

Grey, our lord and savior, was at least able to catch the smallest of scents. He's been spending most of his time with Cora so he was bound to get some sort of hint. He told Lara and I every detail that he could muster about everything other than what we actually needed to know, but finally got to the point eventually. Cora said that they did used to know Ezra, and that they were childhood friends for many years but lost contact years ago, long before he left for Korea.

Cora also states that they didn't know Lara was his sister; they knew that he had one but never met her. I was aware that Lara spent most of her childhood in and out of hospitals, but the details that she gave in the past were sparse, and I wasn't about to dig for information. Well, more than I already was.

According to Grey, the last time that Cora and Ezra spoke, Cora realized that he had turned into a horrible person.

He had always been power hungry, they said, and he most likely went to seek it through means it might be best not to know. Cora didn't seem to miss him, or even care about him, based on the things that Grey told us. If I were them, I probably wouldn't either. If he was already power hungry as a child, then I would hate to see what he's like now, especially knowing that he became part of a crowd that likely made it worse. The real kicker of Grey's interrogation was something that I thought I would never hear out of Cora's mouth. They said that they regard Ezra as being even worse than E, keeping in mind that Cora believes their brother to be the personification of hell on earth; this really wasn't comforting. If that hurt me to hear, then I can't even imagine what Lara felt. Cora said that they're glad he's gone, and that they hope he never returns.

For Lara's sake, I hope he never does either.

I hope for a lot of things.

For instance, I hope that my plan for today works. Tyl has been my saving grace for these last couple weeks, more so than I can even explain. I told Grey to explain what has been going on with my memory to Tyl, because even though I should have been perfectly able to do it, I couldn't get myself to physically admit it. After Tyl found out, being the angel that he is, he has been visiting me almost every single day.

He brings me grapes.

And, to my deepest gratitude, he never mentions what Grey told him. When I said to him that I knew that he knew, Tyl simply shook his head and continued on with a different conversation.

No one knows about these visits, even though I would be alright if they did. I know that I would get many offhand comments from Lara and Grey, but I could handle it. Like I told them before, Tyl and I are friends. Neither of us wish to seek a different label, and this was affirmed fully throughout his visits and all of the many conversations that we held. Though neither of us went too personal, it was never a good time for that, we spoke about our likes, our dislikes, past stories, so on and so forth. We are both incredibly different and incredibly similar, and we find a sort of comfort in that. He's a natural leader, someone who knows his worth but yet not to the extreme of ignoring everyone else's at the same time. He sees the beauty in anyone, in any situation, and he makes it known. Me, on the other hand, though I might want to be the leading type now, I've never been put in that position. I've never been asked. However, similar to him, I do think I can see beauty in all of the same places, in all of the same people. At least, I try my best.

Except for one person, but he doesn't count. I don't think he believes beauty to exist.

Nonetheless, Tyl and I would never work in a relationship, he knows that just as much as I do, and I'm grateful for that. I haven't known Tyl for long, but I don't need time to tell me that I want him as support by my side, and we don't need to be in a relationship to have that. We are perfect together, so long as 'together' means friends.

My Tirn buzzes in the depth of my pocket, grounding me back to the present. I had messaged Tyl to ask him if we could meet at Paul's so that we could talk. He, after all, is the only other person I can think of that might have some answers. Tyl and Cora seem to have known each other for years, which leads me to thinking that he has to know something.

Up until today, it hadn't felt like a good time to ask about Cora. I loved the conversations that Tyl and I had, and I didn't want that to change. I just wanted to talk about life, the good parts of life, and nothing else. But now that we seem to be hitting a standstill in terms of answers, I think it's finally time to at least try to see if he might have answers.

Maybe I'm only grasping at straws, but straws sound better than nothing.

"Hey," Tyl finally responds, "I'm sorry, I can't today. My mom. Bad episode. Have to look after her and Lynia."

I set the Tirn on the table so that I can type more quickly.

Shit.

"I'm really sorry, Tyl. Can I help you with anything?"

I never know what to say in situations like this.

I did mean it though, that I wanted to help him. I wouldn't have asked him to help my stupid plot if I had known this was happening.

Maybe I'm a shit person.

Maybe I'm not.

"No, that's okay, thank you though. How are you today?"

I smile despite myself.

See, he shouldn't be asking about me. He doesn't have to. Tyl has better things to worry about, nicer things, and I've told him that.

He disagrees. Every time.

His mother has had health issues for years, Tyl explained to me during one of our talks, though he didn't go into detail. I don't blame him. I likely wouldn't want to talk about it either.

After a couple more messages of thanks and wishes, I eventually shove the Tirn back in my pocket and collapse on my bed. I don't have work today. I'm not seeing Tyl today. I don't have classes today, contrary to my parents' beliefs. I don't even know where Lara and Grey are. Maybe I should sleep. Eat? Drink? No. What's the use in that anymore? There's not, that's the answer.

Maybe that's the answer for a lot of things.

But there is still one answer left; or perhaps he's a question.

A question that doesn't seem to have an answer. But, I mean, how are you supposed to answer if you can't even find the question. If the question is nowhere to be found. If on the surface you don't even want to think about this question again, but deep down, there's some type of urge. Some type of pull that you can't ignore. No matter how hard you try. No matter how hard you attempt to push it out of your mind.

What can you do?

I guess you just have to look harder.

Fine.

I'll find him.

I'll try, at least. I know that it's not a guarantee, but either way it's a win-win for me. If I can't find E, then I don't have to speak to him. If I do find E, then maybe I can finally get somewhere. Finally know something.

Getting up carefully from the bed, I shuffle my way to the closet. The light burns, causing a brief slowdown in my mind. Maybe none of this is real. Maybe it's a dream. Honestly, I hope so. I can see now, though, so that's a start. I pull out a thin black shirt and pants, chains crisscrossing around the legs, and a dark red corduroy blazer to counter the chill outside. I don't have to grab any jewelry; I fell asleep with a lot on.

That actually could be the answer as to why my ears are burning.

I don't usually sleep with earrings in, multiple racing up my ears. Nor do I sleep with approximately five necklaces on, one of which has left multiple indentations on my chest.

Wonderful!

With surprising ease, I exit my home.

My parents were awake, but they didn't say anything. I didn't think they would.

They don't say much of anything anymore. Not since they got back. I don't know what to do, how to help. How to tell them it seems as if I'm losing my mind.

I guess the simple answer would be to simply not say anything at all.

I like that.

At least the air feels good out here. That's what I'm focusing on. The air. Nothing else. Walking too, actually. Trying to walk quietly with boots on isn't exactly easy but I am however successfully at getting closer to the edge of the forest, so it's okay.

Everything's okay.

E told us that he walks here a lot, and that's basically the only lead I'm going with. My only guide.

I take a deep breath, mentally preparing myself for having to deal with him. *For the pact.* I sigh. I wish that I could have just spoken with Tyl, I wish that his mom was okay, and I wish that I didn't feel selfish for wishing anything like this. I wish that I didn't feel selfish for wishing I was okay. But, again, I'm not focusing on that. Instead, I must focus on the air. Walking. The trees.

Maybe he won't even be here.

I stop. I'm too close to the shed. Way too close. The trees blow lightly in the wind, activating the sound of the wind chime. It is peaceful, I have to admit. A small leaf flutters down and lands on the toe of my boot.

Inhale.

Exhale.

I wish I could stay here.

Forever, maybe.

But alas, I cannot.

I mean, if E isn't here, then why not investigate the shed? If someone catches me then I can play dumb. "I'm sorry, I was just exploring," or, "I'm just a bored teenager," even, "Petrichor owns it? That's cool, sir! My parents work for Petrichor!"

Ugh.

I used to be able to say things like that, but now, it makes me want to throw up. I can't even think about Petrichor without thinking about my parents. How they came back empty. Different. Without thinking about that notebook, the one that I had supposedly been shown at Tyl's house, stating that they're likely the cause of that black smoke. This shed. Without thinking about all of the other people losing their memory throughout the city, and Petrichor not releasing one goddamn statement about it. Without thinking about everything that E claimed.

Maybe I have changed for the worse. Maybe I haven't.

Before I can decide, I'm standing two feet away from the wooden walls.

That was easy.

My brain slows once more, but this time it's accepted. My muscles begin to relax, shuttering against the chill of the wind.

Inhale.

Exhale.

Suddenly, water splatters against my cheek and I look up. A grey cloud has stretched across the sky, and the rain immediately begins to fall.

I don't remember the last time it's rained.

A week? A month?

Pulling the blazer tighter around my body, I walk towards the front door. If anyone asks, I walked into the shed to get away from the rain. That's innocent enough. But, either way, I don't think anyone is here. Maybe I wouldn't even know, though, considering the state that my mind is in currently. Why is it so cold, my mind repeatedly asks. Why are the trees duller? Is the sun brighter? It feels like I can't focus on just one thing, that the world is mixing and blurring and I can't do a thing to stop it. It's been feeling like this for two weeks, like I'm both outside and inside my body. That I am no longer myself, but somebody all the same yet completely different.

That is, until, I feel something close around my forearm that forces my mind into focus. I whip around as my nausea grows to even new heights, and my arm is quickly being pulled around the corner towards the door. Unsuccessfully, I try to pull away, try to run, try to do anything, but all I manage is to knock my head against someone's chest, my back pushed against the wall.

Through my panic, my delirium, I finally make out a face.

E.

I yank my arm away from his grasp as he backs up by a foot. I am too close to him. Way too close.

"Was that really necessary? You could have just said my name, as opposed to grabbing me like you were a fucking murderer."

"Ah, you've learned a new insult? It sounds good coming from your mouth. Something new."

Even despite the joking, his gaze is firm.

"What are you doing here?" He asks.

My eyes squint at him against the rain.

He doesn't seem to be doing any better than I am. E's clothes aren't soaked, but his hair is plastered against his neck, his forehead.

I never realized how long his eyelashes are until now, when the rain sticks to the ends; eventually running down to rest on top of his upper lip.

E raises his voice in a sort of rude panic, "Answer me."

Before I can help myself, a small smile turns at the corner of my lips.

"I was bored."

He sighs, a muscle tightening in his jaw, "Likely. You look like shit. What happened to you?"

Anger begins to rise, not out of offense, but out of his presence in general. I do look like shit, I know that. He, to be honest, does too. Pale. Purple bags under his eyes. Sleep-deprived.

"So do you. I could ask the same question."

I can tell that his anger matches my own, but it only fuels my fire. I have never felt like this before. This anger. This hatred. This confusion. This is the type of hatred that should be gained after years of knowing someone, not days. Hell, not even weeks.

E purses his lips as he slides his hair back, murder with a tinge of sadness in his eyes.

"I've been gone, I didn't think I needed a correspondence with you and your group about every moment of my life. Now answer my question."

"My group?"

"You're the ringleader of the circus, no? The one they all look up to? The light in the darkness? An angel—"

"Hardly," I scoff.

I always believed it was Lara and Grey, the leaders. I usually just go along with whatever they choose, but maybe that'll change. Maybe a lot will change.

"Seems like you are." He smiles a bit, or at least close to a smile. Without happiness. With full menace.

I ask him whether or not it was a compliment, and that short smile quickly turns into a malicious grin. I know it wasn't a compliment. I don't particularly care.

"Only if you want it to be," he answers, his gaze moving from my eyes towards my hands. They've been shaking since . . . since sometime. I don't know when. He raises his eyebrows a bit, that grin only growing wider.

"Scared, angel, or cold?"

I shove my hands deep into my blazer pockets. Neither. The answer is neither. Well, maybe cold, but that doesn't matter. Whatever the reason is, it is not because of him. Nothing is because of him. Honestly, I'm far from scared at the moment.

"Do you want everyone to hate you?"

I know that I had a plan coming here, or rather, bits and pieces of a plan. But plans can change. This question has been bothering me for a while. Does he want to act like this? Does he enjoy it? Does he know the feelings he raises in the people that he speaks to?

E takes a step closer, "That depends. Is it working?"

I swallow.

Yes.

"I think it's your ego, plain and simple. That's why you hate Tyl so much. You feel him as a threat."

E cocks his head.

"A threat? A threat to what exactly? I could quite honestly not care less about your love life."

There it is again. My love life. I didn't even have to mention it.

"Then why do you act like that towards him? Since the first time you met him, you used me against him. In the metro? All of it. Obviously, there has to be a reason. Why join Ignite if you hate the leader? If you hate the members of it?"

At this point I'm practically screaming.

E laughs. He fucking laughs.

It sounds like deep bells in a silent forest. The type of bells that guide you towards home, that tell you where you are, and where you need to be.

"Do you think that I want you? Is that what this is? Do you think I say the things I say because I'm jealous? Huh? Answer me, Meira, I want to know. Do you think that I'm so fucking desperate to the point that I would fall in love with you? That I'm doing all of this for you, joining Ignite, dealing with my sibling?"

And with that, my anger disappears in a flurry of moths. Or at least, that's what it feels like. Not butterflies, but moths. I feel narcissistic. I feel broken. Because the more I think about it, the more I realize that there's a bit of truth to what he said. I did think that E was jealous of Tyl just based on the way that he treats him. The way he consistently brings me up in front of Tyl. Our friendship.

I don't answer, just stare. Stare at his eyes, trying to find any hint of a mask. Any hint of raw emotion.

"You hate me," I whisper, moving closer in hopes that E budges.

He does, backing closer to the trees.

"You hate me, and I know that. I want to know why."

This ignites something within him, loathing, I believe. At least it's real. E's eyes gleam with something similar to his smile, something that causes the same reaction in me.

He searches my face, gaze landing on one of the necklaces I'm wearing.

"Where did you get this?"

Emotion clouds his voice as he reaches a scarred hand towards my throat, but I don't move.

I refuse to move.

E lightly grazes my skin as he holds the small key, the one I've worn since before I can remember. I don't know where I got it or who gave it to me, I just know that I've always had it. I don't know why I can't move. Why I can't stop staring at his hand, his eyes, his face, his hair.

"I don't know," I admit.

E lets it go, yanking his hand back almost as if he touched a flame. The rain falls harder now, extinguishing any sort of fire that might have been there before.

"You didn't answer my question."

E shakes his head, rubbing his hand over his face with an exasperated laugh, like the bells have been cracked.

He touches a shaking finger to the key once more, "Because you, Meira, you . . . are like goddamn *torture*."

Before I can respond, before I can even think, he leaves me standing there and walks into the small building.

The shed, how can he just walk in there? How can he say something like that and just simply walk in there? And here I am, standing alone with more questions than I came with, soaked, cold, and confused.

What the hell did he mean by that?

Fuck this.

I take all of the energy I can muster and storm into the shed after him.

"You can't just fucking talk like that and then leave and-"

And there's a blade to my throat. Crimson red. Blood red. Glowing.

Her crying slows as she moves to look into my eyes. She puts her hand on my cheek.

"You stopped."

I nod, "It's done."

"Do I have—"

"You don't have to anymore," I whisper.

She smiles slowly. That smile. I fall for her every time.

I pull her closer, feeling her warmth. I doze off . . . and I believe she does too.

I push the dream back. This is a dream. Right? This is a dream. Maybe none of this is real? I feel like I'm drowning.

"I said it—" he inhales with a shaking voice as a pain like no other floods my shoulder, "—and now we both have to live with it.

Chapter Seventeen

April 24, 2073

7:30 AM

"I want to show you something," Izmene states, holding my hand and guiding me towards the record room. Or, at least it looks like Izmene.

No. Izmene had long hair.

This woman has . . . I can't tell. The length is constantly changing. Her dress is switching between colors, the brightness increasing as we near the room. As she turns towards me, I recognize her face.

It is Izmene.

It is her. But she's bleeding.

Her nose is bleeding.

"Your nose—" I observe, feeling her fingers tighten around my hand.

"This is nothing. Nothing. Don't worry, you weren't supposed to see that, let's go."

Izmene laughs as blood leaks from her mouth.

Grey blood.

As she opens the door, an immense heat escapes and knocks me backwards, yet straight into Izmene's arms.

"Don't worry, I got you." Her face is set in a wide grin, and suddenly I can see where the blood is coming from. The grin continues to grow wider, ripping at the seams of her mouth.

The sound it makes causes me to almost keel over.

Her grip tightens around my arms, sending my bruises into an orbit of pain. The more she squeezes, the more the bruises spread.

"Don't worry," Izmene repeats, "I have you. You're okay, Meira, you're okay."

Her voice rising into a hiss, a high-pitched screaming of sorts as she leads me into the room. I can barely open my eyes against the increasing brightness, not of her dress, but of the walls.

They're burning.

Everything is burning.

"Izmene, the walls, they're—"

"Shush Meira," she interrupts, "sit."

Izmene motions to a chair in the middle of the floor, flames lapping at its legs. A small table sits next to it, a record player frantically spinning on top, emitting a sound similar to Izmene's voice. I squint my eyes to look closer, specifically to the needle. It's sharp, extremely sharp, fully to the point that it's wearing new grooves into the vinyl itself. Before I can focus my attention elsewhere, I am pushed into the chair as the fire begins to flirt with my shoes.

I am overcome with the sense that this is the end. That I will no longer inhale. That I will no longer exhale.

But for some reason my body refuses to move, the flames spreading bruises over my skin as they crawl up my legs. I can't see Izmene anymore; she's disappeared, and so I'm left alone. Left in a burning room as the noise of the record player burns my hearing, the heat blurs my vision, and the pain refuses to let me move. I am stuck. I am stuck, and utterly lost.

"This was your choice, you know."

Chapter 17

An unknown voice sounds behind me, a slight comfort from the sharp ringing of the vinyl. I attempt to turn around but something, or someone, grabs my head.

"Stay still."

I swallow frantically.

"Please, angel, you wanted this."

Fuck.

E appears out of the corner of my vision, hideously beautiful, holding a needle about the size of my forearm. He smiles as I try to calm my breathing and focus on anything but him.

I can't look at him. I can't look at his eyes.

He tilts my chin so that I'm forced to match his gaze, forced to watch as his eyes begin to bleed the same grey blood as Izmene's.

"E, please, I—"

I can't say anything else.

I can't focus on anything but him. E has trapped me, the flames dancing across his eyes. I can smell the scent of burnt flesh and I dare not look down at his legs, or mine for that matter. I want this to be over, whatever this is.

Please, for the love of god, let this be over.

E stabs the needle through my skull, emitting a soft crack as I am finally released.

"Don't worry, angel."

My mind explodes as I urge into a sitting position, coughing and choking until my mouth becomes dry.

Everything burns.

Everything.

It takes me longer than it should to realize that I'm not on fire, that my body is relatively intact, though not exactly useful. I don't think I can move, at the very least open my eyes. I'm too scared. I'm too scared to open my eyes and find that it was all real, or perhaps that it wasn't and I'm just simply dead.

I don't know where I am, who I am, what's happening to me. *Who's* happening to me. What's real and what's not.

Anything.

Everything.

Don't worry, angel.

Don't worry about what? Don't worry about the burning in my forehead from where E had just supposedly stabbed me with a foot-long needle? Don't worry that when I finally just opened my eyes, I'm on the damn forest floor? Don't worry that I can't remember why the fuck I'm here, how I got here, or why E was in that god forsaken nightmare that I just partook in? Don't worry that I remember a wisp of a knife to my throat, but I can't remember the context? Was it E? Was it part of the nightmare? Was it even a nightmare?

I inhale, breathing in the earth and the morning air.

At least, I think it's morning. It feels like morning, the sun shining through gaps of leaves. But, who am I to say?

I remember I came into the woods for a reason. To find E, and I had. He said something to me, I know he did, but it feels like my brain is trying to block it out. Trying to shove it down until it disappears.

I guess it worked.

But it was morning then too, and yet the sun is still rising and the air is crisp. Maybe that means I haven't been here for long. That Grey and Lara aren't worrying, aren't scheduling a doctor's appointment as I lay here.

Shit.

Crunching a leaf between my fingers, I hoist myself up to my knees, combing the rogue pine straws out of my hair.

My whole situation comes roaring back to me all at once.

It's too late for denial. It's too late to not admit the fact that something's wrong, I can't do it anymore. I know this. I know this but yet I can't face talking to anyone about it. Stressing anybody out. I can't. They have enough to worry about. *Everyone* has enough worry about. If I add onto it, I'm just . . . I don't know. I really don't know. This shouldn't have to affect anyone but myself, and I want it to stay that way. I don't want people worrying over me. I don't want pity. I don't want to feel helpless anymore. I know that I am, I know that I know nothing about what's happening to me and why, but it should be up to me to figure it out. No one else. I'm not a child. I'm not a dog who forgot where its bowl is, where it buried its bone.

I can't be.

Not anymore.

This is my problem, and I will find a solution.

Myself, no matter how scared.

And as of right now, I'm so fucking scared.

But, quite honestly, I shouldn't be thinking of this. I should move. Get up from the ground and wipe the caked dirt from my shirt. From my skin. From my hair.

The fabric is damp to the touch, but there is no sign of past rain. No sign of water whatsoever.

When I saw E, when he said . . . something, it was raining. I know it was raining.

Fuck.

That means it's been long enough for all of the rain to dry, for there to be no hint at all.

Part of me wants to curl up and cry, to stay right in this spot and never move. Never have to face anyone ever again. This seems to be the easiest option, considering that my body feels like it's holding on by a thread, a thread that has been unraveling increasingly as my mind turns on its last hinge. This part of my brain stalls me, keeping me in a sitting position, refusing to move. However, something has changed recently, and I know I have to listen to the other part of my brain. The part telling me to get up and figure shit out myself. My body will forgive me one day, as will my mind, if I continue to move forward.

Forward.

What exactly is forward if I can't even remember backward?

Where do I even go?

I want to be alone, this I know, at least.

I would say the best bet for that would be my house, considering that my friends won't be there unless they know I'm there, and I'm willing to bet anything that my parents aren't there. I can be alone. I can sleep in my bed. I can go to work tomorrow or even today, depending on what time it is, and know that the record room won't be on fucking fire, which is a good start.

As long as that nightmare was truly a nightmare, but again, who can say I can trust myself.

First, I need to stand up to fully get my bearings. Baby steps.

The pain only multiplies when I attempt, but I am shockingly able to succeed and check the time on my Tirn. 7:45am.

Seventeen new messages.

Six calls.

I'll check them when I get home.

Away from this place.

Away from everything.

It's one excruciating step after another. I hobble along as the grass squelches beneath my feet, grounding me. I guess it did rain. For a while, by the looks of it. I wish I saw it, heard its whispers while I drifted to sleep, not worried about a thing. None of which are true, obviously, but it doesn't hurt to wish.

Maybe.

At least I am getting closer now.

I can see the faint outlines of the houses, the solar panels shining with the light of the rising sun. It would be a good picture, if I had my camera. I'm not sure if it would exactly catch the light in the right way, but maybe that would be the beauty of it. Just the thought of returning home to my pictures gives me enough motivation to project myself forward, taking longer strides and ignoring the pain that it brings. Maybe it feels good. Maybe I can trick my brain into thinking that this is helping me, that all of this is gonna make me stronger in the end, like those stories of old where the hero only gets stronger through their perils. A nice sentiment. I don't think I'm a Greek hero like those stories seem to portray, but it would be nice to think. To wish. Anyone could agree to that. However, as of right now, I feel like the goddess of spring. What was her name? She was forced to become the queen of hell?

Persephone.

I feel like Persephone.

"I really think we should—"

Shit.

You can't be serious.

"Meira? Oh, for the love of god!"

I don't exactly think that god is here at this particular moment, but she seems to be the only one. Maybe I missed something. Maybe my parents decided to throw a party with almost every person that I fucking know.

My body is still wedged between the front door and the frame as my eyes scan over the scene in front of me which, mind you, is the exact opposite of what I wanted. What I needed. I very much did not want to be faced with whatever the hell this is.

Grey, Lara, Izmene, Cora, Lynia, and Tyl all look back at me.

The latter is the first to react, pulling me fully through the threshold and into a tight embrace. I breathe him in, thankful for anything that helps ground me to reality despite the situation. Tyl smells like rosemary and sea-salt, the epitome of beauty, a god amongst men like always. I believe that every person alive would wish to be loved by him, but yet, I don't think he knows or cares.

I've seen the way he looks at Grey.

"Please, don't do that again. Please." Lara sighs.

I lean back, "What?"

The rest of the group is silent, Izmene standing a fair distance away from the others. They're not telling me something. I can see it in the way Grey shifts on the couch uncomfortably as Lara stands behind him, fixing her plaid skirt.

I can feel a lecture coming.

"Meira." It was Izmene this time, switching places with Tyl. "You disappeared. Two days ago."

Blinking, I attempt to stifle a laugh, but it's unsuccessful. I said I wasn't going to worry, that I was going to fix this. I said that this doesn't affect anyone other than me. The thought still remains.

"I messaged Tyl yesterday morning," I smile, moving past the onlookers to take a place on the couch.

"The day before yesterday," Cora whispers.

I try to refute, but Lara interrupts, "Meira, please."

I never told them to come. I never asked for any of this.

"How did you guys even get in? My parents—"

"Are not here." This time, Grey. He continues, "I made sure, before I walked in. I came to find you. The door was unlocked."

I stare at him, "And everyone else?"

Grey doesn't answer, he doesn't need to. He told them he couldn't find me, that I was gone, and they all showed up here, in my house, without my knowledge. I shouldn't be angry; I know I shouldn't. They care for me, they're here because they were worried about me and they didn't know what else to do. Why am I angry? Why can I not look any of them in the eye without having an urge to leave?

No. I know why. Because this is real. Them being here shows that it's real; it's not just affecting me anymore. They are trying to tell me this, and I hate it.

I hate all of it.

"Where were you?" Lara asks, her voice soft.

See, that's a very good question.

"After I messaged Tyl, I went to the woods as a shortcut."

Lies.

"Because I wanted to fix my camera."

Liar.

Screw it. There's no use.

"And then," I sigh, "I changed my mind. I decided to go by the shed. I had stories made up for why I was there in case it is Petrichor that's involved. I remember that I got there, and then it all goes blank. I woke up on the ground, the only difference being my arms."

Once I got started, I couldn't stop; I didn't even want to mention the part about my bruises. Luckily, I refrained from mentioning E. It felt like a good idea, as it almost seems like he's close to being forgotten.

"Your arms?"

I swallow, staring at Cora's face riddled with suspicion.

"What about them?"

Honestly, I wouldn't know. Moving to one of the chairs, I let Izmene roll one of my muddy sleeves up, a small gasp escaping from her lips. After hearing this, the rest of the group crowds around to observe the damage. I feel like an animal at the zoo, trapped and suffering without knowing why. Well, I'm not sure if zoo animals suffer; I've never been to one. I'm not even sure if they exist any longer. If they do, maybe the animals there thrive, it's a nice thought.

"When you woke up," Cora rolls my other sleeve, "they looked like this?"

My gaze remains glued to my lap, not wavering through the questioning, "They've been getting worse, slowly."

"Do they correspond . . . with the memory loss?"

This catches my attention. *Do they?* I attempt to think back to the first time I remember something not fitting, it was something small, barely noticeable. A clear plastic bag, I believe. I didn't question it then, but I am now. Question everything, they say. The plastic bag, a small bruise.

Forgetting how I returned home from Paul's, the bruises spread. Forgetting most of everything that happened at Tyl's house, the blue turns to purple. Today, my shoulder is covered in them, the process beginning on my other arm as well.

"Yes." I look between Cora and Izmene. "I think so."

"You woke up near the shed, in the forest?" Izmene.

I nod.

Horror. Malice. Understanding. The glance passed between the two of them, grandmother to grandchild. They realized something unanimously, something that I haven't yet.

"Cora?" Grey asks.

But it's too late, the fire in their eyes is too strong for Izmene to fight, marching to the door in a rage of fury.

"He's dead, I swear to god he's fucking dead!"

And then Cora is gone. Just like that, causing a wave of silence in their wake. No explanation. No hesitation. I can only assume that Cora is speaking about their brother, as he seems to be the main cause of their anger. The only one not here. How he has anything to do with this, I don't understand. I don't want to ask. Not right now. Not after that.

But something in my brain is screaming.

"Let's go, Meira. Okay?"

Tyl moves to support me as I stand from the chair. I never should have sat down. I lost all form of energy when my muscles relaxed; as much as they could at least. Lara and Grey shift to help as well, Lynia is staying put. I don't blame her.

"Wait, Grey, stay with me," Izmene sighs. "We'll wait for Cora."

He swivels his head between Izmene and I, shooting me a low thumbs up. I raise mine as well which results in a huge smile on his part, one that I can't help but copy. Izmene is right, he should be here when Cora returns. That is, if they decide to come back. If not, it would likely be because they're out burying E's body with multiple dagger wounds.

I never thought I would say anything like that, truly.

With the help of Lara and Tyl, I was finally able to make it to my room, settling under the covers of my bed.

"I wish that I could stop this," Lara intertwines her fingers in mine. "It shouldn't be happening. Maybe we should take you in, the doctors would know. I mean, it's their job, right?"

I smile, slightly squeezing her hand, "It'll be okay, I think. I'll see a doctor. Just not right now, not with everything."

It's not a lie, necessarily. Doctors probably could help, and maybe I will go in eventually. But like I said, not right now, there is too much happening. Too much with Petrichor. Too much. Hell, we haven't even been able to focus on the invisible shed portion. It seems like the least of my worries.

"You're symptoms . . . some are close to a few of my Mom's."

With one look at my expression, Tyl knows to continue.

"Mostly memory loss, gaps in life, things like that. Not the bruises though, that's unique to you." He gives a little wink.

So maybe I'm not psychotic. It isn't just me, this time. Little lights start to go off in my brain, twinkling in the usual darkness; it's funny, sometimes, how one simple thing can make someone feel so much better. Unification. Representation. Relatability. I never noticed how much I needed these three until I drew the short end of the stick. I knew that there were some families of Ignite members that were going through this as well, but to know that someone closer to me, someone who I supposedly had met is going through this too . . . it's nice, in some twisted way.

Lara runs her hand across the pictures on my wall, "You know, I think I'm starting to miss . . . huh, what was her name? The one that wouldn't shut up in Ignite, caught Meira in that long conversation at Paul's?"

"Grace," Tyl exhales a short laugh, "Who, by the way, is actually one of the people like you, Meira. It's not just her granddaughter anymore. She started to remember odd things and forgetting others; they even looked into a dementia diagnosis, but the doctors didn't think it was right."

"Maybe I should talk to her," I reply. "Or," correction, "she should talk to me."

This causes a hearty reaction from Lara, laughing as she walks towards my door, "You're mean now, you know. I'll be right back."

I smile, leaning my head back against my pillows, happy to not be lying in the dirt anymore. It was peaceful, though, in any case.

"If you want, when you're feeling better, I can help get the mud out of your hair."

"It's okay," I yawn. "It's really the least of my worries. But thank you, Tyl, I'm glad you're here."

At this moment, I almost feel normal. I almost feel like I have a common cold and my friends came to visit me, to make sure that I'm okay. In this made-up world, my parents would be downstairs, watching TV and waiting about ten minutes before checking on me again. Grey and Lara would be playing match-maker, Tyl laughing as he plays along. Cora would be there too, and even though I can't say I know them extremely well, I still have the urge to get to that point. To know about their life, their childhood, what happened between . . .

You know what, he's not even in my made-up world.

E would destroy it anyways.

"When Cora stormed out, do you think they went after their brother?"

Tucking away my paradise of a world, Tyl's question remains in the air.

"I assume so."

He sits down at the end of my bed and cracks his knuckles, "Do you know why?"

"No," I admit. It's true, I don't. Yes, I did go to find him. Yes, I remember speaking to him. No, I can't remember anything after that. I can't even remember what he said. What I said. How Cora knows that he's involved, I'll never understand. I mean hell, maybe he isn't and it's all just one big coincidence.

I take a deep sigh, pulling my necklace out from underneath my shirt and twirling the chain around the key.

"Where did you get this?"
"Answer me."

Dropping the chain, I press my palms against my eyelids. What the hell was that?

E never said that to me, but yet I can hear his voice in my head as clear as day.

"I said it . . . and now we both have to live with it"

When was this conversation? I feel like I'm being taken over, slowly losing myself over and over again.

"Meira?"

"I'm okay."

Tyl ignores my lie, moving closer to pull my hands away from my face, "Are you remembering something?"

I explain it to him in briefest detail. A conversation with E, one that I can't place. He was asking about my necklace, and that's the only context I have.

"Did you go to the woods to find him?"

I can't look at Tyl without feeling a sense of regret.

"Yes, but it was out of curiosity."

"One would guess," a smile plays on his lips, "or hope, maybe."

Very true.

But was it really curiosity? Or was it something else, something I can't remember, some distant thought in the back of my mind that I can't place? Something that I might never understand, something that I'll never know?

"Hope what?" Lara asks, returning with a bowl of noodles. I freeze, glancing at Tyl.

Please don't tell her, I attempt to mentally convey.

"Hope that Cora won't come back to us as a newly proclaimed murderer."

Time after time, I am constantly racking up debt to Tyl.

A savior, of sorts.

"Why would you hope that? I personally wish that I could join Cora."

A laugh of relief escapes my mouth. I trust Lara, I really do. I just don't trust that she'll believe when I say I went to E out of curiosity. I'm not even sure if I believe myself.

"Besides the dream of murdering that son of a bitch, even though I don't know what he has to do with this situation, I assume that you're hungry," Lara hands me a bowl and sits at my desk.

Food, huh.

It seems like a foreign concept, something that I know I should want to eat, but can't. It's horrible, and I never know how to explain it. My body feels like it's being weighed down by the lack of nutrition, especially in recent events, and I don't know how to stop it. I don't know how to be better. 'Better' for the lack of a more descriptive word. In the old world, things such as this used to be glorified. 'Under-weight' was not always a bad thing, and that horrifies me. We learned about it in school, the social norms, so that we know what not to repeat. For once, it seems like the world wants to fully work towards not repeating history. Finally. But, nonetheless, what I have is not glorified. It's not something that I want, but it's something that I'm stuck with. In times like this it only gets worse; but maybe after it's over, if it ever does end, I'll work to enjoy something that I know I should enjoy.

Maybe I'll finally start to feel better.

"Don't want it?" Lara asks, finding me staring at the bowl in deep thought.

"I do."

Tyl slowly takes it from my hands to set it on the bedside table. "Don't force it. You can eat it after you sleep a bit."

Lara seems to agree, which makes me feel better. I don't want her to think I'm not appreciative, but as she leaves my room with Tyl behind her, the look on her face tells me I don't have to worry. The hint of sarcasm always helps.

"Sleep, you don't have to find an explanation just yet," Tyl smiles with a brief nod and closes the door behind him.

An explanation. Not just yet.

If there even is one.

⁜

I don't even open my eyes. I don't react. There's no need to. Being woken up by yelling seems the most normal event out of today's catalog, if it's still even the same day. I'm not exactly sure how long I've been asleep, but I also very much do not want to check.

What's the use?

Time already seems to be sweeping me off my feet, better to be ignorant with small things like sleep.

I don't exactly feel like I've been asleep for long, even though my body does feel a bit refreshed, as much as it can be.

Sleep still mists over my eyelids as I try to tune into the raised voices. It doesn't sound like a painful scream, which is why I was barely phased, but it's definitely not a normal tone. Two tones, actually, two voices. I can't exactly hear what they're saying, but I can tell who I think it is, especially in context.

The loving siblings reunited again.

I shut my eyes fully, pulling the covers up to my chin.

It's freezing.

"Nope, absolutely not," Tyl bursts through my door, locking it when he enters. "Not happening."

I believe he's talking to himself.

He pauses, glancing between me and the locked doorknob and

raises his hands, "Sorry, not trying to lock you in, I just don't want to listen—"

"It's okay," I laugh a bit, even though it likely came across as exhausted. Tyl nods as he sits at the end of my bed again, head collapsing into his hands.

"Is Lynia still downstairs?"

"No," he sniffs, "luckily I was able to take her home before all hell broke loose."

Hades and his sibling.

I should ask Tyl how his mother is doing, but I assume he doesn't want to focus on that. The fact that Lynia was able to go home without him being there hopefully tells me that she's doing better.

"They found him?" I ask, the bitterness in my voice shining through.

"No, he just showed up," Tyl replies.

So, I was right.

Was it likely that he showed up willingly? Absolutely not. Not with Cora here, Tyl and I as well.

"Voluntarily?"

He shakes his head, "Cora convinced Izmene to send him a message somehow. Obviously, whatever it said worked like a charm. I'm not sure how Izmene did it, Cora said that E doesn't have a Tirn."

No, he'd rather steal them off of innocent bystanders.

"How long has he been here?"

Tyl moves, laying his back against my bed, hands still covering his face. This is the most relaxed I've ever seen him. Well, maybe not relaxed so to say, but with a comforting lack of traditional politeness. "Too long," he sighs. "The moment he walked in, Cora was already up in arms. We separated them, thankfully, before it got worse. E looked like he was going to kill Cora when he realized he was tricked into coming here, whatever they messaged him wasn't true. I came in here because they want you to come down, and I disagree."

"I'll go."

Finally, he reveals his face, the evident lack of normal glow throwing me off guard.

His eyebrows crease in worry, "You can barely stand, Meira. I'm not the type to constrict people but I really don't think you should."

I attempt to test my muscles by moving closer to him, a bit sore but nothing far from the usual. Despite not knowing why, I know that they're arguing over me. Tyl doesn't want me to have to deal with that, and I understand, but I need to know what's happening to me, what they know and what they're not telling me. Izmene and Cora both realized something when they saw my bruises but they don't want to explain; I can see it in the way Cora watches me, the way that Izmene watches me. Maybe E is just a pawn, someone wrapped into the middle of something he didn't expect, someone that just wants to be left alone. On the other hand, though, there's a part of my brain, cracked and unwanted, that holds a constant stream of longing. When I hear unknown voices or unknown memories, they come from this broken fracture, and E seems to fit right in.

"I need to know what's happening," I stand, holding out my arms towards Tyl, "Will you come with me?"

A smile of disappointment prickles Tyl's lips, reluctantly taking my hands to help both of us up, "Yes, unfortunately."

"Tyl is right, it might have been better for you not to come down here. Cora told me that they wanted to bring E here to simply talk,"

Izmene strains a laugh, "and I actually think they were going to try if not for E's immediate reaction."

Funny, Tyl said the exact opposite.

"Where are they?" I ask.

"Cora is outside with Grey and Lara . . . we put E in the side room."

I nod, eyeing the closed door to the right of the kitchen. My chest constricts a bit, breath quickening as that door becomes the only thing I can think about.

I need to go in there.

I need to go in there and ask what's happening and why Cora and Izmene reacted like that and why I can't get him out of my mind even though he—

"Go," Tyl whispers in my ear, "just call if you need me."

Inhale.

Exhale.

Half thinking, I give him a thankful smile as he continues the conversation with Izmene, my feet leading my body without trying.

Should I want this?

Should I not feel ashamed for the changes in my brain when I realize that E isn't just a myth?

That he's not just a character I made up in my nightmares?

But yet I can't stop myself from resting my hand on the doorknob and praying that undoubtedly, he is in fact real, that my memories haven't abandoned me one last time. That my hatred towards this person is tangible, and that he holds the same feelings.

That he is the answer to so many questions.

As I walk into the room, I let the supposed hate fuel me and course throughout my blood.

Chapter Eighteen

April 24, 2073

11:30 AM

Almost immediately E rushes towards me, his hands switching from lightly touching my face to gently holding my arms, "Meira, they . . . they told me . . . I thought you were . . ."

I stare at E, startled by the gentleness of his voice.

The overwhelming worry in his gaze.

His touch.

E looks softer now, the darkness of his eyes less accentuated by the light purple splotching below them.

I guess that neither of us can sleep.

That neither of us can do much of anything.

He stares at me as if I'm his reflection in a pool of water, his eyes moving in a triangle from each of my eyes to my lips.

"What are you thinking?" E asks, careful with every word. I focus on the dark grey color of his sweater, wondering if he continues to dress like this even when the weather climbs in temperature

Too suddenly, my mind caves in on itself.

"You said that I was torture, you touched my necklace . . . you . . ."

My ears are ringing frantically as my mind races. I force my legs to remain standing.

His breath catches, "What?"

What?

"What did I say?"

At that moment, I see the small amount of color drain from his face as he moves even closer to me, "You just said something, Meira, please."

My frustration spikes in the wake of his desperation. I repeat once more that I didn't say anything. I didn't. Fuck. I didn't, right? Swallowing, I shut my eyes, a pounding throb beginning behind them.

"I made a mistake," he whispers frantically as he squeezes my arms at my sides, "*someone* told me to do something and I listened, I listened and I shouldn't have but honestly I really couldn't have said no. I wanted . . . I—I needed . . . Shit, Meira."

He continues to speak but I can't hear him.

I can't hear anything.

Someone.

"—and Cora lied to me, they said you wer . . . it doesn't matter, and now I'm here and I want to kill them. Simply."

I stare at him.

"They want you dead, too."

The corners of E's lips turn up a bit in a small smile.

"So I've heard," he says.

E lets go and I lean my back against the door, in part to listen for voices and also in part with mental exhaustion, "What was your mistake?"

His breathing is uneven.

"The past. I should have left it as such," E looks me up and down, locking me still with his sharp gaze full of pain. "Hate me, please. Hate me as much as your friends do, my sibling, Tyl, I suppose. Hate me like you used to, when I could see the anger in your eyes. It would make this easier for the both of us."

God, I wish I could.

I wish that I didn't see him in the way that I do now.

Scared.

Worried.

Desperate.

I feel like I'm being smothered in fabric, falling incredibly fast into dark endless waters, him being the stone that drags me deeper until he's finally holding me close.

"I can't."

E's eyelashes flutter slightly as he tucks stray curls behind his ears, shocking me with the realization of how young he seems at that moment. I can hear the conflict in his breathing, the quiet rustling of thoughts behind walls he keeps locked tight.

The urge to tell me everything and nothing at all.

E doesn't look at me, "Why can't you hate someone that already hates you? All of you, Meira, every goddamn inch, every word. Every time you look at me I just . . ."

If it wasn't for the sole fact that I'm the only person in this room, I would have thought he was addressing someone else.

But all it takes is one look into his pain-glazed eyes to see that hate is a substitution.

Hate is a mask.

Hate is not real.

"I do hate you, but not in the way you want me to," the words begin to spill, "I hate you because I can't. I hate you because I can't tell what

I'm seeing when I look at you. I've never felt like I know so much and so little at the same time. Yet you know what's happening to me, I can tell that you do. Izmene and Cora have their suspicions but *you*," my partially silenced mind takes over and leads me, moving closer only so that I can grab his limp hand and close it around my necklace, "*you know exactly what's happening to me, and so much more.*"

I leave E standing there, the key of my necklace burning against my skin as hot as my sudden anger, "Get Cora, we all need to talk. I'm done with secrets, I'm done."

I slam the door behind me.

Bad idea, I'll admit.

"They're bruises, Cora, what the hell do you think I have to do with this?" E yells.

Grey grasps Cora's hand, likely trying to calm them. Izmene sits next to me as a sort of mediator between the opposite couch and E standing behind us.

"You disappeared for two years," Cora raises their voice only a bit, "and when you unfortunately decided to come back, this shit starts. You knew the risks; you knew what could happen if you did this but yet you just had to do it anyway. If you really cared, E, you would have listened to us years ago and you could have actually helped us. How many times do I have to tell you to leave it alone? It's too late."

"Cora," Izmene tries as I tilt my head back to look at E.

His glimpse flickers to mine only for a second, "Why are you doing this, here, now? You try to tell me the risks as if you're not walking the edge too, doing it like this."

I thought they would explain. I thought all of them would explain. I thought they would all see my desperation to know and would tell me.

But no.

Only more secrets.

"Please," I practically beg, "please just tell me what's going on. If you know what's happening to me, I feel like I have a right to . . ."

I'm interrupted by E as he moves from around the couch, crouching to be eye level with his sibling, creating tension that is unmatched. None of them answer my pleading.

Of course they don't.

Looking between E, Cora, and Izmene, something starts to bloom inside of me. Fear is the closest word that I can think of, though I've never felt it at this level. Even looking at Tyl doesn't help the growing feeling to ease. Grey and Lara are my only respite from the new wave of nausea, my vision blurring to the point that it's kaleidoscopic. Izmene doesn't notice, fully focusing on her grandkids on the brink of war.

"I wished that you lived with me. You wouldn't have to deal with them." He giggles, twirling a strand of his hair. "I wish."

Voices crawl through my mind and escape through my eyes in the form of involuntary tears. Not crying, not laughing, something far from it. I can't tell if it's a memory or a dream, maybe a mix of both, but the voice that spoke came from a young boy full of affection. I could hear it in his tone, in the barely legible glint of his eyes. My own are closed now to block out the real images in front of me, the yelling that I can hear increasing.

They haven't noticed.

"I'm okay, I really am. It was an accident. They didn't mean to," the boy says, wind blowing softly through his long hair as the sunlight radiates around him like a halo.

"I know, but maybe I should wrap it again."

He shakes his head and lifts his newly covered hand into the sunlight, "It's fine, see? Not even a speck of blood." He smiles, and I melt.

Stop. This isn't real. There is no golden boy. No. Maybe if I sleep more, eat more, think more, then everything will be okay. I'll be okay. The golden boy's hand will be okay.

"I wrapped it well enough, right?"

My eyes focus again on my living room, waiting for an answer.

"What?" E turns towards me, now standing.

"Your cut," I reach for his hand and he complies, letting me run a finger over his scar, "It healed so quickly."

And then the world slows.

"It did, Meira, it—"

The darkness slides in. The walls fall.

"Stop, E, don't go along with it. It doesn't help," only echoes. All echoes.

"Hey, can you hear me? Meira? No, please, I'm so sorry. I'm so . . ."

⁂

No.

I like who I've become, I do.

Looking back at who I used to be feels like a chore, a mess that I have to clean, leaving past stains. The stains are persistent. I try my hardest not to let them bleed through, not to show anyone else the crumbling memory of a forgotten person in the depths of my mind. When I'm alone, unfortunately, these ruins build back up again, even if it's only slightly. The hatred comes back, the blissful ignorance, the disappearance of happiness that I can only refer to as the natural state of things. My chest constricts, tears forming but not falling, a lack of motivation to help myself, much less seek out the source of these conflicts. Especially now, after going so long without building up a tolerance to it, I'm not sure how to act. Do I let the tears fall freely? Do I sit here and think and only make it worse? Or do I try to fix it? Ignore it, maybe? Let the feelings convulse and interlock until they're overflowing in a waterfall of deprivation. God, how easy it would be just to slip right back into that. I feel as if I've been balancing on a trip wire for weeks upon months and it would just be so much easier to fall. Fall back into the past, into the easier place, that godforsaken, horrible place.

But I can't, and I won't.

Eventually I resurface from the drowning water, grasping for breath. A tight squeeze envelops me as the kaleidoscope becomes clearer; my senses begin to evolve again. I'm on the floor, I think. No better place to be, huh? I start to laugh a bit, mentally, not physically. Haven't gotten the hang of moving muscles yet, but we're getting there. Someone is holding me, and I feel like a baby. Fetal position, head resting on whoever's chest.

"You're okay, I promise." The voice is close to my ear.

"What's happening, Tyl?"

"She's coming back, my mother does the same thing."

Tyl. Tyl is holding me, I can see his silhouette through my squinted eyes. I'm facing the door and I think Grey and Lara are behind me, based on the two different hands on my shoulders. Cora crouches in front of me, Izmene somewhere else, and E . . .

"Don't even try," Cora looks past me, "don't fucking touch her. Don't speak to her."

I guess E is behind me. Not for long, though, as he strides for the front door, taking one last look at Tyl and I before slipping out and leaving silence in his wake.

⁘

"Don't worry about work for a little bit, not until you feel better," Izmene smooths out my covers, speaking softly.

"Thank you, I'll be back soon I hope."

She nods, the last one to leave. Tyl left first, reluctantly, after I was able to stand again. He had to get back to his mother and likely repeat the same process over again. Grey and Cora were the next to go. They probably wanted time alone, I would too if I were them. Lara was the last before Izmene. She took back what she said about seeing a doctor; if I have the same thing as Tyl's mother, then there's no use. They all said they would drop by until my parents come back; I tried to contact them again, but nothing. I'm scared for them. But the feeling is almost like a wisp. Whenever I even try to think about them, my brain numbs itself, switching to a different topic.

And god, do I fucking hate that topic.

Chapter Nineteen

May 21, 2073

2:00 AM

It wasn't worth it. Whatever it was, whatever I did, whatever I chose to get myself into this position, it wasn't worth it. And I know it was me. I can feel it. I can see it when I look into the mirror and only recognize half of myself.

I've thrown myself to the wolves.

Honestly, I hope that E's the cause of all of this so that I can support Cora in whatever endeavors they would like to go on against him. I wish that it's him so that whatever feelings—whatever I *think* about him is fucking gone.

No one has even heard from him.

Almost a month has gone by.

To be fair, I haven't seen Cora either but at least I know that they're still located somewhere on Earth. Izmene says that they're extremely busy right now but they continue to ask how I'm doing, and Izmene always says *better*.

That's where I disagree. Ever since I had gone missing last month, I've been put on "house arrest"—I wouldn't necessarily describe this as *better*. Who suggested it? Lara suggested it, Izmene advocated, and then the rest of the team is managing it: Tyl, Grey, Cora from the outside, and sometimes even Lynia.

With these newly established "laws" put in place and no parents to stop them, even though I doubt that they would anyways, I'm stuck. Yes, that's right, my parents are still not back. No contact. It's not as if there's something spreading throughout the city, causing a multitude of memory loss and confusion cases very similar to someone I just so happen to know very well. Or half, maybe. Petrichor has taken notice of the cases and is beginning to look into it, so they say.

I don't think it's true. I think they're avoiding it, besides some bullshit public announcements.

Avoiding any fear that their citizens might be having.

Shoving it under the rug.

If it was true, I think I should know what's wrong with me at this point.

That Petrichor would have told me. Told anyone.

How did I even get here, making up theories like this?

I don't know, truly, but it's a bit fun. Nevertheless, things are beginning to happen, I guess. Petrichor has sent out information via Tirns. I don't have custody of mine at the moment—shocking I know—but Tyl keeps me updated when he visits. Apparently Petrichor is also reaching out to doctors, brain and other specialists. If it's for a possibility of a suspect or for innocent help no one knows yet, but I bet we won't know anytime soon. Tyl says that he's worried about his mother too. She keeps searching through the notebook, the one that I supposedly looked through as well, but I wouldn't know, would I?

Grey and Lara seem indifferent, the former more devoted to the issues within his own relationship than caring about a theory. He still wants answers, of course, just not these specific ones, I wish that I could help him more, give better advice, but I have very little experience in the matter.

Tyl has told Grey to talk to Cora multiple times; he says that communication always seems to help situations of confusion. What better way to know what a person is thinking than to ask them? Wouldn't really know, but I trust Tyl. Grey swears over and over again that he's tried to talk but he can't reach Cora, which to me sounds likely, with a hint of sarcasm. I can understand not being able to get a hold of them, but the questionable part is whether or not he actually tried. Grey and confronting issues are like poorly attracted magnets, they know that they're supposed to attract one another but they just can't seem to get the motivation to see it through. I'm sure there's a logical reasoning behind Grey's disgust of attempting to fix issues, probably having to deal with bad experiences of said attempts in the past, but I don't wish to bring up old wounds unless I absolutely have to.

Speaking of old wounds, the 'fits' as Izmene likes to call them, are happening more frequently. You know, the dreams or memories or whatever the hell they are. In fact, they are starting to feel less like dreams and more like a memory, even though I can't piece myself into them. The best way I know to explain it would be to imagine watching a movie in your childhood, and then in the present you suddenly remember one of these vivid scenes. You've seen it before, you know it's not a dream, but yet you know that you have no way of fitting into the events of that vivid flash.

I've started calling them flashes, only in my mind. Making a term for it makes it seem less foreign, I think. Maybe Petrichor should start using it and putting a nice little red bow on the little shit storm that people are facing, pretty it up for them. The government has been a bitter topic for me recently. I mean, I'm surrounded by people that have quite the vendetta against them, what did you expect? Not only that, but when you're on "house arrest" for almost a month you start thinking, which leads you to questioning, which leads you to forgetting and then questioning again until you wish that you could stop thinking until you reach an opinion and . . . then you're screwed. Maybe these thoughts can act as revenge towards my other half so that she can be hurt too, finally.

Breathe. Stupid fucking advice. I'm breathing, I am. Too much. I would like to breathe less, my throat constricting between sobs. I don't know how this happened, I don't exactly want to know, but it's here and I can't—I can't. My room is completely dark yet it remains spinning as if I've hit concrete and decided to down four bottles of vodka. The tears came out of anger, I do know that, but as for where the malice came from . . . I don't know. The anger led me to hatred. Pure. It began to drown me as if it was asked to be here, a welcome friend that thought it would bring me a gift for old time's sake.

Well, fuck old time's sake, and fuck this gift.

I can feel my damp pillow against my ear.

I want it gone.

Gone. Lost. Dead.

My throat aches, searing pain whenever I attempt to swallow.

I need to get up.

I need to leave.

How do I do this? Can I walk if I'm spinning?

Sure.

I need to count, I think, that will help. When I get to five, damn it all. Easy.

One.

I grasp the blankets, clenching my teeth.

Two.

Hoisting myself up to my elbows, the blood rushes to my head and I want to throw up and I want to lay back down and I want to sleep and I want to—stop. Stop.

Three.

I'm sitting up.

Four.

My feet lightly touch the ground, legs dangling over the bed.

Five.

"Five songs?"

"Yep," he answers, tracing a figure eight on my palm. "Tell me."

The leaves are still above us.

"Um, what about some of the ones I played for you yesterday? I can send them to you."

The golden boy turns his head away as the wind picks up and sways the tree.

"Sure, I can learn them."

And I'm on the floor. Where was that? That flash? That tree? *That* tree. The park.

I decide I'm going there.

I need to go. I need to go and figure out if this is a dream or a memory or something completely goddamn different. Dragging myself up off the floor is no easy task, my energy draining like an hourglass. No one comes to visit me this late at night. It's late, isn't it? It's dark outside. Close enough. Maybe I can watch the sunrise with whoever my mind continues to drift to, leading me on like I'm some type of puppet. Well, whatever it is that's happening, it's working wonders on me. I'm on the stairs now, shuffling more than walking. Considering that I still feel relatively terrible, I would say that I'm gaining well. But, on the other hand, the front door stands in the way like a looming guardian.

"I'll be fine."

And I'm out.

The outside air causes me to pause on the lawn, realizing a bit too late that I don't have shoes. I fell asleep in sweatpants and a ripped tank top, but no shoes. Definitely no shoes.

Fuck it.

It's too late. I've already started to walk.

The asphalt is cold to the touch, the smell clearing my head a bit. It must have rained recently. If I could only smell one thing for the rest of my life, I would choose the scent of rain hitting asphalt, what else? The sound comes as a close second, the peace that comes with every drop and as my bare feet walk against the cool pavement; I feel like I can almost hear it. The peace, though, I cannot feel. Maybe times have to be simpler, simpler than whatever life turned out to be.

I, personally, never thought I would be struggling to walk in the complete darkness so that I could eventually board the metro to the park. The park in which a tree sits that might hold the key to unlocking some sort of sick and twisted reality where I feel content.

The golden boy, who lives in this reality, seems to be causing me more harm than even my other self, wherever she may be. Maybe she's in the same place that she puts me when I'm being thrown away, hidden from any answers that actually might help me fix things. But that would be too much trouble, wouldn't it? Keeping me in the loop? Absolutely not. Luckily enough, however, I am able to lose track of time as I'm thinking, feet are slowly becoming rawer as I approach the quiet station. The glass door slides open, providing me with one last checkpoint before I finally decide to do this.

I don't feel fear, the unknown anger has almost dissipated, and my energy seems to have peaked in the night air.

Yet there still remains a problem.

I don't wish to evaluate exactly what that might be at the moment, but at least I know that even if I did, I likely would not succeed. No reason to doubt that. Does the problem have to do with the fact that I have heard noises behind me ever since I left my house, but yet I refuse to turn around? Perhaps. Why can't I turn around? Because I'm doing something. I'm going somewhere. I have a goal in mind, and who are we without goals? Exactly.

As I walk into the station, I am immediately pleased with my decision. There is not a person in sight, the only noise is coming from the low hum of the metros themselves, no longer any mysterious sounds behind me. Double checking my observation, I board one of them, not bothering to check the stops.

I'll get there eventually.

The doors close slowly and I'm safe from any indecision.

A moment of peace.

I close my eyes, leaning my head back against the window.

I hear the footsteps first.

Heavy.

I refrain from opening my eyes, unaware of how long I've been asleep. I judge not long, based on the fact that my eyelids still remain dark. The inside lights would have turned on if sunrise had hit yet. I don't attempt to catch a peek. If they think I'm asleep, then they won't bother me.

"I need to speak with you."

Maybe they're not talking to me.

Maybe they're talking to the other me.

Maybe they're talking to the golden boy.

"Your eyelids are moving. Open your eyes."

I don't recognize the voice.

I'll be at the park soon, I will be. I'll get off soon and I won't have to deal with this.

A sharp pain in my shin forces my wish to halt, eyes shooting open. I look for the source of pain first before anything as my hurried gaze lands on the tip of a boot, covered in metal.

"Look at me."

A hand forces my head up, face to face with someone unknown. His hair catches my attention. A dark buzzcut, two lines shaved near both temples. At first glance, I would say he looks to be about five or six years older than me, a narrow face with overgrown stubble. He releases his hand which allows me to look at the full picture. His clothes are minimalist, a steamed white short-sleeve shirt with dark dress pants, no wrinkles in sight.

"You're interfering in something that you don't understand, can't understand. You have something of mine in your bloodstream,

I can see it in my sensors, an excess of it, but yet you're flying in and out of the radar. I need to know how and why. Speak."

I don't know what happens, what causes it, but I start to laugh. Slowly at first, growing as the situation begins to set in.

"Who are you?"

And why does he look so similar to Lara.

He refuses to answer.

"I'm just trying to get to the park. If there was anything in my bloodstream, I think I would know about it, quite frankly."

No, I wouldn't.

He leans back, a shadow darkening his features as he turns his head to the side. The longer I analyze his features, the quicker I realize how screwed I am.

Ezra.

It . . . fuck.

It has to be him.

"You're not supposed to be here."

He turns back towards me, nothing but anger concealed in his gaze.

"My sister," he practically spats the word, "is wrong about many things."

The fact that he didn't feel the need to say Lara's name shows that he knows who I am, that he knows more than I do.

The churn of the metro mimics the hum in my ears.

This is what I wanted.

Ezra has to have answers, to something. There's a reason he sought me out. Why he's intertwined with Cora and E.

This is exactly what we wanted, right? I mean, I didn't expect answers to come straight from the source, but I would say this is a bit more efficient.

"You used to be friends with Cora and their brother, and then you left for another country. Your parents didn't even know if you were alive or not. Why?" I ask, looking straight at him.

This seemed to have hit a nerve.

Ezra stands, the full height of him looming over me. I can't break eye contact, I can't show that I'm scared or even worse, conflicted.

"They can all burn in hell. This planet would be a better place for it." He runs a hand through my hair, roughly pulling it back and locking my head in place when I try to move away. "Your parents, on the other hand, were supposed to help me but yet they gave me absolutely nothing. They have no idea what you're doing, do they?"

Anything that I say, anything that I do has the chance to tell Ezra exactly what he wants to hear.

He wants to hear that I know.

"I don't know what you're talking about."

A muscle in his jaw tightens, "I've made them forget everything that I asked. I can do the same for you, let you forget the pain, the confusion. Let you go back to being a normal family, like things used to be, hm? Just tell me what you did, or if not, then who did."

Who did.

Like I would know, like I would know anything.

"Why did you ask my parents instead of me? I'm the one you're accusing, not them."

Ezra rests his right hand on the arm rest, leaning over to the point that I almost feel suffocated.

He's too close.

Too close.

"Your mind would not have been able to take it. It wouldn't have worked, you're corrupted. Your parents, though, were perfect."

If my mind can barely handle this, then maybe he's right.

He says that I have something in my bloodstream, and if I do, a lot of things might be explained.

Everything.

Without warning, his left-hand slithers from behind my head to my mouth in one swift motion, not giving me enough time to react. Panic spikes as my heartbeat roars in my ears. I need to get out. I try to wrench away from under him but a dull pain spurts in my wrist, causing my gaze to flicker. He has a hold of it, squeezing so hard that his knuckles begin to turn white. I try to release the hand covering my mouth with my free one but it's no use, the harder I try the more he tightens his grip. Even attempting to kick has no effect, his metal-tipped boots holding both of my feet down. I am completely and utterly stuck. Tears spill down my face as I continue to try and twist and turn away from his grasp.

Please, just kill me.

I don't know what I did. Who I am. What I did to fucking deserve this? Deserve any of this.

"It's a shame . . ." His right hand moves to my knee, leaving my wrist a limp mess, and begins to move up my thigh. "Having you with me would have made someone very, very upset. What I wouldn't give to see his reaction to this moment. But," He sighs, "work always comes first. Let me know when you're willing to speak, but if not, let this be a warning to you, or if you're just a pawn, to anyone else involved, old friend. To let them know how much I missed you."

Darkness begins to slowly take over the edges of my vision. My muscles cease to function, my hearing quieting to a buzz. I can't move anything except for my eyes, landing on something protruding from my side. A mahogany hilt, glowing red.

Ezra straightens, taking the knife with him, and I can hear his footsteps farther and farther away.

He left.

My mouth opens and I begin a choked laugh as my head droops down to my chest. Why am I laughing? I try to focus on the muscles in my face and I slowly determine that I'm not laughing, I'm not crying, it's something far different. Suddenly, my blurred vision hones into the side of my stomach where a small flower of red begins to bloom.

I need to feel it. Blood. Any way that I can.

The tips of my fingers grow numb as I take all of my effort to move them to the red stain, slick and wet. I swallow as I stare at them, now covered with red as well. I can't feel anything anymore. No pain, no confusion, no anger.

All too soon, my eyelids flutter, and everything ceases to exist.

Epilogue

May 23, 2073

3:30 AM

Maybe if I-

I can hear wheels screeching.

I could maybe move-

Now the lurch of something being carried.

I don't think I can-

Huh.

Something has been locked. Two of something, I hear it.

A quiet beep. Another. Another. A rhythm.

It begins to speed up. Each beat the tempo increases, I feel it.

I can't stop it.

Maybe if I-

Light comes first, fast and unwavering. The room settles around me as if a curtain has been opened. All white, the ceiling. Hearing comes next, the steady trill of a machine. I can feel my fingers, my toes, my eyelids, my—

I jolt, sitting up faster than I could have ever imagined. Not my wrists. I can't move my wrists.

I'm strapped to the bed.

No, no, no, not like this.

I yank as hard as I can on both of the straps, the side of my chest burning like hellfire. *Please*, a small scream rips through my thoughts, *I don't want this*. My vision is hindered again, eyes clouded with tears and hearing blocked by sobs. I should have never left. I should have never left the house and got on the metro.

I should be dead. I really should be dead.

"Hey! Hey," a tight embrace consumes me as I continue to struggle with the restraints, "Meira, please. Hey! Don't do that, please Meira—I . . . it's okay."

My energy runs out quickly, wrists aching from the strap burns.

I stare at Tyl.

"Where am I?"

He doesn't let go of my hands, "Safe."

My breathing steadies, not because of peace, but because of anger.

"What are these?" My eyes flick to the restraints and right back towards Tyl. He licks his lips carefully.

"Precautions. There's been cases, Meira, of people having the same symptoms as you and then hurting themselves because—"

My voice is cool, "You think that I did this to myself?"

Tyl looks away, likely startled by my tone, "It was a quick assumption. You were found alone in the metro; your hand was on your side. We did what we thought was right."

"Take them off."

He doesn't move.

"Tyl."

He doesn't speak.

"Take them off."

"No," he runs his hands through his hair. "Not unless you can tell me every single thing that happened."

My gaze wavers, a small sense of betrayal peeling at my skin.

"Fine. I wanted to go to the park and I decided to take the metro."

"At three in the morning?"

I ignore him, explaining everything before sighing deeply, ". . . and then Ezra left me there to die."

Horror creases Tyl's brow as he blinks. "Do you mean Lara's brother, Ezra?"

"Yes," I whisper.

"Meira, as much as I trust you . . . I . . . Ezra is in Korea."

I shake my head.

"Not anymore."

He is here. He is back.

"I think that even if—"

The door opens.

"—Ezra was back, what would he want with you?" Tyl finishes before glancing at the noise.

A heartbeat.

Another.

"Can I speak with you?"

My mouth opens slightly.

I don't know how much he heard, how long he waited. E looks like an exact replica of desperation. His hair is in a bun, an emotionless expression on his face as his gaze lingers on me.

"I don't know if—"

"Yes, you can," I interrupt.

Keeping steady eyes on E, I feel Tyl squeeze my hands as he stands up. He stops right before the door and whispers something into E's ear before leaving. His expression doesn't change.

"What did he say to you?"

E sighs, pulling the side chair closer to the bed, "A threat."

I didn't expect anything else.

"I was told not to come in here, but I needed to see."

His voice is something I can't explain. It draws me in to the point where I almost forget who he is, sitting next to me like some sort of unknown past.

"What are these?" he asks so softly, running a hand over one of the wrist straps.

"Precautions," I whisper.

"Fuck that," E shakes his head as he carefully begins to undo the buckles. "Fuck them, you don't need them. God, you were fucking stabbed for fucks sake! They should actually be trying to help you, not whatever the hell this is."

I watch every move of his fingers, every deep breath that he takes until he removes both straps, leaving one of his hands to rest on mine.

"I shouldn't have—"

"You don't usually—"

We both stop, staring at each other with eyes full of exhaustion.

He tells me to go first.

"Why are you acting like this?" I turn towards E, careful with the hospital gown.

"Like what?"

"Agreeable."

He smiles a bit.

"God, who knows."

As I move, I feel some sort of bandage stuck to my side and my hand instinctively slides out from under his.

I was stabbed.

I mean, I knew that I was stabbed but . . . it didn't feel like reality. Can someone even come to terms with that?

"You should wait before telling anyone that works here about what happened. I don't think they would take being wrong lightly."

I close my eyes as a bolt of pain shoots through me, "I just want to get out of here."

"That makes two of us. Let's go."

Should I? No. *Am I going to?* Uh, yeah why not. I don't want to be around people who blame me faster than anything else. I'm not saying it was Tyl's fault, he likely had nothing to do with it, but these doctors, *Petrichor*, they bound me before even hearing my story. Before understanding anything. They would rather blame me than themselves. They would rather blame me than admit that a crime was committed in their own metro.

Fuck that.

"Do you know where my clothes are?"

E pauses in the midst of helping me up, "You're right, you might need those," and lowers me back down.

I watch as he bolts through the door until his footsteps are no longer audible.

This is about the exact opposite of what I was expecting: E acting as if he's a real person as opposed to an enemy to all. He looked completely normal up until Tyl left and then it was like he snapped. I think he guessed everything that happened between Ezra and I based on the way he was looking at me, of course, only if he heard what Tyl said. He had to have, right? I mean, he walked in right when Tyl said Ezra's name. And besides, every time E looked at me his eyes screamed, "What else did he do to you? What did he say?"

Too much, is what he said.

Besides the evident wound in my side, I also have to deal with Ezra's words. With more confusion.

With the fact that E almost sounded *protective* over me.

However, at the current moment, I can barely even think straight.

I feel highly drugged up.

Highly.

I move my hand under the hospital gown to feel the bandage taped to my skin, which seems to be doing a very good job at the moment. Shifting to my other leg, I lift the gown fabric for the first time to truly look at the consequence of curiosity. Only a small drop of red has bled through the bandage, something that I consider to be a win. Starting to heal, maybe. Modern medicine.

The door slams open.

"Oh thank god you're up, I need your help. Do you remember that store that I told you about—oh, first off, how are you feeling?"

I cover the discarded wrist straps with a blanket, "Good, Grey. I'm good."

As much as I can be.

"Good, I'm glad because that shit was uh, it was terrible. Likely more for you than it was for us but you know, scary."

"How is everybody else?" I ask.

How are the doctors that strapped me to this fucking bed?

Grey loosens his ponytail, "Eh, you know. I don't know."

"This is all I could find," the door opens once more, "they got rid of your other ones. Bloody. Hopefully these will fit." E ignores Grey, setting a pile of clothes on my bed.

"What are those? Weren't you told not to come in here?"

E puts his hands in his pockets, "I don't recall."

This seems to be a continuous trend, E being places he shouldn't.

"You definitely were. Get out," Grey straightens his posture. "I highly doubt she wants to see you any more than the rest of us."

"Oh, I beg to differ," the other grins a bit, a slight flash of a sideways smile.

Please, I silently beg, *Grey don't start.*

Why did E have to say it like that?

His eyes grow wide as he points two fingers at E and I, gasping as dramatically as possible.

"You can't be serious," he whispers, impressively loud. I shake my head and continue to explain just how wrong he is.

"I don't believe you."

E is having too much fun with this, "The girl was stabbed, Grey, am I not allowed to speak with her?"

"I don't think 'just speaking,'" Grey and his air quotes, "warrants bringing her clothes. Whose even are they?"

"Mine."

Oh perfect.

"Yours? Yours. So, nothing is going on but you're perfectly fine with Ira wearing your clothes?"

"I thought ahead. Assumed she would need them. You know, considering hers are no longer able to be worn, but it seems like I'm the only one who thought of that."

This causes me to look away, attempting to remember why I hated this boy.

"Assumed she would need your clothes, not her own?"

"Mine were close, no one else seemed to have offered. Maybe

someone was having too much fun with their significant other to have even cared that their friend was hurt? If I'm not mistaken, I believe I was here before you were."

Ah, that was why. The wars he starts and then leaves behind. Something that I'm all too familiar with.

"You don't mean that!" The golden boy mutters, refusing to look up.

"If things were different then maybe I wouldn't, but they aren't, and you know that better than I do."

And just like that, he leaves.

My eyes become dry from lack of blinking, the rest of my body at a standstill. I can only hear Grey's voice through a mental filter.

"Really, is that right? Ira, do you agree with him? Do you think that I didn't care?"

I can't answer. The flash still lives vividly in my mind, causing the world and my memories to flip upside down.

"Fine." A hazy Grey stomps out of the room, the noise of the door slamming, echoing throughout my nerves. My vision goes blank.

"Don't slam that damn door!" A young teenager with long hair yells in a deafening scream that could make blood curdle.

"Fine, let's go. We're doing this ourselves. He doesn't think we will, and that's our advantage. Lock the door."

"Fuck, Meira. Please, not right now. Not right now. We'll go back and I'll fix this and we'll—hey, can you see me? Can you hear me?"

My muscles twitch in small spasms as an immense amount of pain wracks my body. I would almost feel like I'm entering death if I had never felt this before. Worse than death. E's face shoots to a focus, the worry and pain in his eyes enough to cure hatred. His mouth is parted into a forced smile, hands cradling my head.

"You can see me?"

"E?"

"Just focus on me. I promise I'll take this all back and I'll explain everything just please hold on Meira, hold on. Don't do this again."

The world spins once more as, a flash of light crosses my vision and I hear my voice speak.

"Erebus, is that you? How is this happening? I think I love you."

My eyes flutter . . . and I am gone.

About the Author

Raidin is a student at UNC Chapel Hill, majoring (as of right now) in Journalism and English. When she's not writing, she's typically reading or playing music (she's in a band, you should check it out, she thinks it's pretty cool). She loves to be creative in any way shape or form, which causes her to have way too many hobbies. Raidin was born in Raleigh, North Carolina and has stayed around that area for her whole life even though she loves to travel. She has a dog named Thriller and way too many plants, all with their own names, which would cause this biography to be way too long if all of them were listed. However, if you ask her about them, she would love to tell you about each and every one of them.

Instagram: @_r.a.i.d.i.n_